STORM ROLLING INTO DARKNESS

a novel

GRAHAM DUNCAN

 FriesenPress

Suite 300 - 990 Fort St
Victoria, BC, V8V 3K2
Canada

www.friesenpress.com

Copyright © 2017 by Graham Duncan
First Edition — 2017

Cover Design by Leah Renihan

All rights reserved.

No part of this publication may be reproduced in any form, or by any means, electronic or mechanical, including photocopying, recording, or any information browsing, storage, or retrieval system, without permission in writing from FriesenPress.

ISBN
978-1-5255-0756-4 (Hardcover)
978-1-5255-0757-1 (Paperback)
978-1-5255-0758-8 (eBook)

1. FICTION, CONTEMPORARY WOMEN

Distributed to the trade by The Ingram Book Company

For Carmen

your encouragement helped carve a way forward.

Because, you know,

some days the well was empty

and your support

was all I had.

THE SWING

I remember that morning. Sun glistened on ripening apples and honeybees gamboled from flower to flower. I stood mesmerized in the backyard unknowingly rejoicing in the perfection of life. How could I know otherwise? I was a nine-year-old girl who only knew how to be happy.

I rose early to explore my tiny tree-lined neighbourhood kissing the edges of the salty Pacific. It was a magical place. Gina, Chelsea and I were inseparable. In the afternoon, like many that summer, we raced to the beach and with tentative steps waded into the too cold ocean before scampering out to warm ourselves against a sun soaked stone wall. Reveling in the simple joy of a vanilla ice cream cone, smooth and intoxicating like the wavering scent of honeysuckle, we tried to make the ever-shrinking treat last until the afternoon heat forced us to slurp the melting remnants.

Later, we chased dogs in the park until exhausted we fell to the ground laughing our guts out as hounds and mutts licked syrupy vanilla from our chins.

And when the night grew dark my friends came up to my place where we splayed in the backyard spying the heavens for celestial bodies. Stars, magical impressions, crystal-like, wavered hypnotically like unreachable gems at the bottom of a midnight blue lake. We laughed at our imaginings, travelling in spaceships to new worlds, strange, enticing worlds where curious and curiouser revelations defied our perceptions.

I was sound asleep when Kate came to my room. She shook my shoulders until I woke and in between gasps she wiped tears away with the back of her hand as she told me Mac was leaving us. I didn't understand. Wasn't this another of my father's business trips? I wanted to sleep.

Kate wanted to wrench out all the pain. Her head lay heavy on my back as warm tears soaked my nightie. Her words faltered, unable to find a way forward, she sat up, clenched my fingers in warm dampness and tried to assure me that we were going to take care of each other. I knew differently. I understood I would be the one to take care of her.

Her girlfriends came over. Kate told them about the breakup. These women who had partied in our home and laughed at the uncertainties of life morphed into a pack of wolves feasting on fresh meat. Their eyes transformed into tiny slits, angry green slits of hate. They called Mac names, told Kate her marriage was over and the life she knew was never coming back.

I hated them.

Kate tried to stop their chaos but simmering bitterness boiled over. She winced. They used words I had never heard before, like shithead and prick, words that rolled silently off my tongue in a glee knowing I was secretly absorbing the intimacies of adulthood.

Outside, a rainstorm slapped the front window. An afternoon darkened. On the floor, resting against the back of the couch in my t-shirt and shorts, my feet stretched out. I wiggled my toes. How odd they looked, like an ancient rainforest creature. I tried to stop my baby toe from wiggling but couldn't. I laughed but nobody heard me.

One woman said Kate should forget about Mac. Walk away, she said, and begin a new life. If Kate walked away where would I go? She urged Kate to go back to school and get the law degree she wanted. Another nervously informed the pack she left her husband and was staying at a women's shelter. It was safer for her and the children. Her voice rattled. I peeked around the couch.

She was a big-boned woman with messy, red hair. She had a black eye. A baby suckled at her breast. I stared. Her blue, wattery eyes glanced my way. I spun around behind the couch and wiggled my toes.

The frightened woman continued.

She said he didn't hit her, often. His threats and sullen glares, these were the silent killers wearing her down. He stared at her through dinner, rage searched for signs to pounce. He never said a word. He ate and she sat perfectly still even when the baby cried in the other room. He wouldn't let her leave the table until he finished dinner, that way, he said, she wouldn't annoy him.

Dinner over, he shoved the plate at her and the utensils rattled to the floor. He liked to throw the fork at her tits, said he liked to see it bounce. He followed her every movement, especially when she cleared from under him, the room silent except his nostrils hissing.

He forced himself on her every night. *I didn't understand what that meant.* Afterwards, she said she lay on the bed afraid to move as he sat on one side and pulled out a cigarette. He was his nicest then, when he puffed and head bowed said he wanted to buy her pretty clothes and take her to Las Vegas. He said she was as pretty as any women he knew. He didn't know why he did the things he did, but she should be careful because he couldn't help himself.

Another woman told Kate she didn't want to end up like poor Cheryl, alone in a shelter. Why would Kate have to go to a shelter? What would happen to me? Why couldn't we stay here? These women never mentioned me. I wanted to tear their eyes out. I wanted to grab Kate's hand and run away.

The rain stopped and I slipped outside where scents of wisteria and delicate roses made me feel better. On my swing, I pumped my legs and pulled hard on the ropes. Climbing higher, pumping and flying until at the peak I saw kids playing in the yard next door.

One of them waved. It was impossible to wave back. I had to hold on. I was moving too fast.

They laughed and shouted, daring each other to make dramatic catches as they threw a baseball back and forth. They waved again and shouted for me to come over. I wanted to, but how could I? I couldn't be like them. I didn't know exactly how, but I understood my world was coming apart. Happiness and the bees were frauds, and I was now like Kate, sad, without promise.

I watched the boys until, bored, I stopped pumping and dragging my feet in the wet grass I hopped off and went back inside.

Another woman, bitter as she was brittle, glanced at me as I slunk into the room. She avoided looking at the others, pulled on her wedding rings, and then looked at Kate and told Mom she had to get Mac back. It was the right thing to do, there were demons in Kate's mind preventing a righteous marriage from prospering with more children.

The woman's voice rose higher. I jammed my back hard against the couch. She told Kate to go to church and pray and talk to her minister. She said Kate must have done something wrong. The room went cold.

I was ashamed of Kate. Ashamed she let herself fall prey to these women who feared the world so much they punished her so they felt better. They stripped her until head down, she wept.

I never forget what they did to her. I never forgot *Shelter-lady*.

For weeks, Kate drifted away. I didn't know what to do. At dinner, her eyes stared without blinking. She often glanced my way and I could see she wanted to say something but couldn't. Most nights, I left my plate unfinished, and went up to my room and closed the door.

And then Mac came home. When he hugged me, he squeezed me harder than ever. I felt odd, unbalanced, dizzy-like. I almost smiled but something inside told me to *Be careful, wait Andie, you don't know if this is going to last.* It didn't.

Kate was angry when I asked if we could be happy again. After that we talked less and less. It was better that way. Unable to cry, a numb feeling slithered into my limbs and an ache in my chest, like a rock against my ribs, throbbed whenever I tried to breathe. One afternoon in class, when Mrs. McAdam insisted we be quiet, the rock pressed hard and I gasped.

I survived. Alice saved me. She understood my wonderland. In time, so did I. Eventually, I remembered the happier times. And vanilla ice cream cones.

LUNCH

Kate walked out on Boxing Day when I was twelve. It was her turn. During Christmas, we went through the motions. Nobody said much. I discovered Anna Karenina. Tolstoy was talking about my family when he wrote, "*Happy families are all alike; every unhappy family is unhappy in its own way.*" Princess Anna's story, however tragic, seemed romantic compared to the life of a pre-teen trapped inside a dispirited family.

After Kate left I made meals, did laundry and cleaned the house when I couldn't stand it any longer. Mac was rarely around. The few times he sat at the table he uttered a word or two about his company and leveraging contacts with the Socreds. He never asked about me. I wouldn't have told him anyways.

Kate wasn't gone long. She came back on a bright Sunday, February afternoon. I just was home from the library, standing in the hallway when the front door clicked open. She stood defeated, plastic bags of dirty laundry trailed behind her. Her rumpled coat, stained and torn on one sleeve hung limp on her body. Her once rich auburn hair had faded to a dusty beige. She needed a cut. She tried to smile. She wrapped her arms around me, her tiny fingers kneading my shoulders as shallow breaths brushed my cheeks.

I kissed her forehead, told her to go and shower and I would make dinner.

This afternoon as I drove downtown to meet Kate for lunch I thought about those days and why we grew further apart. I tried caring for her, and Kate, she tried her best. She tried, but I was changing and at some point I lost her as I was losing myself, and there were times, more and more, I didn't care what the fuck was going on in her life. Maybe that's why all these years later, now Kate and Mac are finally about to divorce, I couldn't give a shit.

From our sidewalk table I glanced on to Government Street as crowds of tourists angled their necks around passing throngs to peer inside shops.

"Andie?"

I looked back absently. "Why now?"

"I should have done this years ago."

"You've never gone through with it before. Why now?"

She sighed. "I think you know. Don't pretend."

I shrugged.

She peered over her sunglasses. "You're not surprised. Don't do this."

I sipped, held the glass to my lips and stared disinterested.

Kate slipped her glasses off placing them on the table. Her pale blue eyes were exhausted. She didn't have it in her. And maybe she didn't need to. In the last ten years, she and Mac hardly saw each other. Both were fully committed to separate lives. Why couldn't they continue this way? Shit, why did I care?

"We've grown apart."

You mean, *you've* grown apart."

"I have my career in a firm that values me for my contributions. I never had that with Mac, that feeling that I could contribute as much as him. From the beginning, he wanted to be the breadwinner. I lived under his shadow far too long."

"Have you, really?"
"Don't."
"Does he know you're going to ask?"
"He's aware of my feelings."
"But he doesn't know you're going to throw this at him."
"Don't say that."
"Is there another man?"
Kate shook her head.
"Someone in the firm?"
"I won't jeopardize my work for a fling that fades when infatuation dies."
"So you have been tempted. Men and women do have office affairs."
"I'm not you, Andie."
I shrugged.
"Are you still seeing Seth?"
"We go for a beer now and then."
"Does he have a real job yet?"
"Your attempts at sarcasm are pointless." I finished the Merlot and signaled a waiter passing by. "Another, please."
Kate was staring at me.
"What?"
"Two glasses for lunch?"
"And?"
"You're teaching this afternoon?"
"Not till three o'clock."
She snatched a buzzing phone, tapped then placed the phone on the table.
"Who is that?"
"The client I'm meeting later. Says he may be early and wonders if I can meet at 2:00 p.m." She glanced back at the phone. "We should order lunch."

I sipped. "I'm not hungry."

"I am."

A waiter arrived and Kate ordered.

"Are you moving out of the house?"

"I have to."

"Where?"

"Downtown."

"Leaving Dad on the peninsula?"

"He doesn't have to stay. He can sell and move to Whistler. He spends most of his time there."

"He never calls me anymore."

"Doesn't he?" Her words were thin.

"I like hearing his voice."

"Ever thought of picking up and calling him?"

I glared. "It's something you used to do until your lawyering became more important."

Kate shook her head. "It's not going to work."

"What?"

"Baiting me."

"It usually does."

"Not today, Andie."

"I thought you liked this as much as I do."

"Life's a game for you, isn't it?"

"Maybe." Smug felt good. Doesn't matter. This was how we got along. And though I didn't like myself much after these sessions I didn't know any other way to get through.

"When are you going to ask him?"

Kate looked up from her phone. She hadn't heard me.

"When are you going to ask Mac for a divorce?"

"After Tofino."

"We're still going through with that shit?"

"It won't hurt to drag yourself out to the coast for a few days."

"I'm bringing Seth with me."

"Suit yourself."

"I don't know why we're going. It makes no sense. Just ask for the divorce."

"The three of us had great times in Tofino."

I scoffed. "When?"

"When you were a little girl."

"That was thirty years ago." I sipped more wine. "The last few times we went for breakfast, walked the beach for a couple hours and then Dad slunk to the bar and drank by himself for the rest of the weekend."

Kate winced. "You and I spent time together."

"I read and hiked. We hardly spent any time together." I got up. "I have to pee."

When I came back Kate had just finished a call.

She sat up in the chair and leaned forward.

"What?"

"Let me tell you something. In life, there will be too few people you will fall in love with. I mean someone you love forever. If you find that person you better grab hold."

"Great advice."

"You know Andie, you're not convincing as a bitch."

"But it helps me get by."

"It's a mask you don't wear well. At some point, you're going to have to start liking yourself."

"Thanks again. I'll keep it in mind."

"I was in love with Mac for a long time. I tried to make it work. I know he tried but he couldn't change."

"His chauvinistic ways."

"He grew up believing it was his responsibility to take care of me."

"Like a pet, combed and fed."

"In the seventies women were prized possessions of male athletes. I thought I could change him. We were young and when we had you, life was good. I was excited to settle into a domestic life. At least for a few years."

Kate's phone buzzed. She moved to the sidewalk, gesturing with her hands, cheeks clenched, head jerking to the sky in exasperation.

When she returned to the table she slammed the phone down and snapped. "What we were talking about?"

"Nothing really." I took a long drink and then casually offered, "Seth has a child."

"What?"

"Rom's almost ten."

"Who is the mother?"

"Her name is Melissa. They were married for a couple of years."

"Why are you telling me this?"

"I don't know."

"Raymond?"

"Rom."

"I'm sorry, Andie. My client cancelled. I have to go back to the office and amend the damn contract."

She tossed her things in her purse, pushed her glasses on and leaned over to kiss me. "Give your father a call. He'd like that."

She was off, dodging tourists as she turned down Fort and out of sight. I imagined her paced quickened when she caught sight of her new Audi.

I gulped the last drops in my glass. A waiter stopped. "I could use another, thanks."

FAMILY

Almost two-thirty. Shit. No way to make class. I texted Alain and told my teaching assistant to have the students review last week's online postings on the state of the Canadian Senate. It would placate them, undergrads more intent on high marks than diving into the dysfunction of the Canadian political system. I couldn't blame them.

Alain's a good man. It's his wife I don't trust. She chose Victoria and she's intent on Alain stealing my position. He's shy and plodding and in the final stages of acquiring his PhD. What am I going to do if he heads home next spring? He wants to take his family back east, Toronto or Montreal, somewhere where cheaper flights to the Maritimes prevail compared to prices here. Not sure his wife is going to let him.

Inside my condo I kicked off my heels and opened the wine cabinet. Out on the deck with a glass and bottle in hand I dropped into oblivion. Christ, it's hot. I emptied my glass. And another. A late afternoon sun wilted the last of my resistance and the glass slipped to my hip as sleep descended.

I dreamt of Rom and his innocent smile and the way he looks my way but never at me. He asked questions about the radio broadcast we were listening to, wanting to know why the announcer articulated some words differently than others. He was so particular, noticing the cadences and emphasis placed on words and certain phrases. I tried answering him as best I could but as the dream shifted to his big brown eyes, he swallowed me whole.

He smiled and I smiled. He made me a part of him. I can't explain it. Maybe it's because autistic children have a difficult time relating to the feelings of others and because I seldom express mine maybe things are easier for us. We played in his room. We laughed. We lay side by side on his bed. No words. Just us. Rom and me.

When I awoke a stupor held me hostage. My face burned. *You should have changed out of your work clothes.* Kate and I had lunch? Didn't go too badly. Ha. Shit. Glad she left early. We'd had our fill. Why does she always feel she must be nice to me? I prefer to be alone.

I drifted along unnoticed in high school, oblivious to classmates and teachers, skipping classes to read in the library, skipping school to read at home where books occupied afternoons and evenings and summers drifted by too fast with multiple re-reads of F. Scott Fitzgerald's *The Beautiful and Damned* and short stories by Maugham.

Hanging out with friends annoyed me. What was the point? I remember when my friends told me drinking was cool. It was grade eight. Going home from parties I watched them puke their guts out on the street in front of their parents' homes. Parties didn't make sense. I drank alone and my problems disappeared. And, the high, I never wanted it to go away. Mac and Kate were seldom around. They never noticed wine bottles missing from the cabinet.

In the fall of grade twelve I read *Democracy* by Joan Didion and spent time in front of the television watching coverage of the

1988 federal election. Everyone talked of free trade but I glommed on to the contrasting personalities of the party leaders. Turner's veneer of sincerity cracked under pressure. Some how he felt the need to apologize for Trudeau's transgressions. He looked weak. He was weak. Ed Broadbent, personable but far too earnest, was the perfect imitation of stammering Dodo in Wonderland. Brian Mulroney, now this guy was a gangster. He'd cut anyone down who got in his way.

It was my first time as a voter and the emergence of the Green and Reform parties made the potential tangle of alliances and the possibility of minority government all the more intriguing. *Remember, you drank in the afternoons? After a few glasses of red you were surprised how easily ideas opened up.* Warm and liberated, my imagination ran wonderfully wild. I had this crazy idea to dedicate myself to chronicling the demise of Canadian democracy in a three-book set. Back then politics meant something to Canadians. Back then politics had a pulse.

I tried pulling myself out of the lounge chair. Needed another drink. My legs flopped to the deck. I reached for the doorframe to steady myself. Opened a new bottle and poured into a clean glass. Mmmm… this floating feeling. *You know you're going to get drunk tonight.*

Lying down on the couch by the open door, I unbuttoned my blouse and slipped off my skirt. Kate's so utterly transparent. She says she cares but what does she do? She grabs her phone, talks to a client and then runs back to the office, ignoring the fact we were in the middle of a conversation—she couldn't remember what we were talking about. All she wanted from our so-called lunch was to announce she was asking Mac for a divorce. Why now? Go ahead, if you dare. Ask him. He'll agree.

Pouring again, glass in hand, I stumbled as I move across the room. Thumbing my CDs, plucking *The Best of Sarah McLachlan.*

Christ, Sarah torches me. "Adia", this is Seth's song. Didn't McLachlan say "... *more than anything this song is about my problems dealing with feeling responsible for everyone else.*"

She was talking about you, Seth.

Sipping. Head back, hair draggling, glass slipping, it crashed to the floor. Shit. Shards everywhere, I escape and flop on the couch. A fog of inebriation rolls over. Mouth agape, eyes closing.

I don't know when, it was dark and numbness in my fingers pricked pain up into my shoulders. Flopping my body around I splayed spread-eagled on my back staring stupidly at the ceiling. Tried lifting my head, spinning, spinning…

Later a cool breeze and laughter on a summer night drifted into the room. And then night terrors—fitful battles with Kate. Don't let her win. Imploring her to abandon her marriage, she sneers, "Mind your own business." Why did she tell me then? Why does Alice always ask questions?

I grabbed a blanket and wrapped it around me. Need to lay this body down. Tired. This fuckin' world's tired.

And then a dream.

Soothing tropical waters and pink and blue corals float by enticing me to follow. The current pulls and fluttering like a dolphin I chase luminous corals in the warm waters. Limp, floating easy with the current, my eyes are wide and curious. I'm a child again.

Then desperate without breath, I swim until the burning in my chest forces me to the surface and the sun assaults. Turning away, wiping my eyes, I peer towards land where two figures, a man and a boy hand in hand, diffused and wavering in the afternoon heat, slip farther and farther away.

HANGING OUT

Seth plunked himself in the chair beside my desk. I turned a page and continued to read knowing his impatience would get to me.

"Umhhm." Fingers drummed the chair. "I thought you said you wanted to go for a beer?"

"You annoy me when you do that."

"Do what?"

"Twitching, fumbling, that shit with your fingers."

"Just trying to get your attention."

"I know. And, I don't drink beer."

"Oh, yea. You're a wine aficionado."

"Don't be an ass."

"And class today?"

"You know what second year poli-sci students are like."

His heavy eyelids lifted. "The scandal in Ottawa is getting juicier. I bet they were tapping madly into their phones in vain attempts to expand twitterverse." He checked his phone and looked up, "They didn't need to listen to you with so much political intrigue unfolding on social media."

"One did."

"You mean your pet."

"Shut up."

"Have you bedded him? Summer term's almost over."

"Shut up. I would never."

"No?"

I closed my book. "You're actually boring when you try to be like me."

"You think he's cute. You told me."

"I'm not interested. Besides, I've got you if I want sex."

"Yea, but when was the last time—"

"Let's go for that drink."

"You look tired," he said.

"Kinda." I walked around the desk and grabbed my purse.

"It's not your usual disinterest?"

"Might be."

"Hardly anyone understands those inscrutable expressions, but they're as much a part of you as your long, curly hair that I adore. Your disinterest might go unnoticed, but not you. The chocolate hair and eyes are unforgettable."

I ignored him and flicked off the light. Seth grunted out of the chair and rumbled behind me down the hallway. The parking lot radiated in waves as the stench of newly-laid asphalt stung our nostrils.

"I'll drive," he said.

"You'll have to drop me off at my condo later. I'm not coming back for my truck."

"Are you teaching tomorrow?"

I nodded.

His head jerked across the road. "My jeep's parked beside your truck."

"You're not supposed to park in the faculty lot."

"As if you care."

"I don't."

It was pleasantly cool in the pub. I led the way to a booth in the back next to the entrance to the kitchen where we were ignored. Waiters rushed by until Seth blocked the path of a kid I thought too young to work here.

"A glass of Merlot and a pint of Sea Dog, please." Seth tilted his head in mock deference then stepped aside. The waiter flew off.

As he sat down I took a long look at Seth. When was the last time I trusted another human being? But this relationship is about hanging out. And drinking. Seth's my built-in excuse. He isn't as strong as me. And I get to hang out with a political hack and part-time cook in faded Zeppelin t-shirts tumbling over ripped jeans unable to hide a bulging gut even if he's a big boned man at six feet four. Jesus, the receding sandy hairline makes him look forty-five, not thirty-four.

"Melissa wants me to come over and fix her cable. She wants to watch Netflix with her new boyfriend."

I sniggered. "New boyfriend?"

"Yea. Another penny-pinching realtor to match her ambitions."

"Why doesn't he fix it?"

The waiter placed drinks in front of us.

"How do I know? What I don't get is who watches Netflix in the summer? They have enough money to tour Italy all summer."

I took a long sip. "I want to go to Italy."

"You do?"

"Don't you?"

He took a drink then put his beer on the table. "Not really."

"I haven't watched Netflix since, I don't know, sometime in the spring."

Seth wrapped a big hand around his beer. "Who has the time?"

I smirked. "You would, if you stayed away from your porn."

He shook his head and looked away.

"Oh, poor boy. Don't look so disappointed."

"Why do you say those things?"

"Have you seen Rom?"

"Not for a couple weeks. Melissa says I can have him on the weekend. I'm picking him up Friday afternoon. Maybe the three of us can have dinner Sunday."

"I'd like that."

"How was lunch with Kate?"

"She met me before a meeting with a client. He cancelled. She left."

"You always pretend your mom doesn't matter."

"She didn't come to see me."

"Why are you so indifferent?"

I laughed hard. "You have no idea."

"Enlighten me."

"It's a difficult relationship."

"I don't get it."

"I don't want to talk about it." I emptied my glass.

"If I had parents—"

"When she and I get together we twist our shit over and over until we're bored or tired or both. She doesn't understand I've moved on."

"And she's not allowed to care?"

"She can do whatever she wants. I've put my demons behind me."

"Demons? Do tell."

"Not a chance. I'm tired of this." I looked around for the waiter. "Mac wants a family get together next month in Tofino. He's booked rooms overlooking the Pacific. Want to come?"

"You're kidding? You know what your parents think of me."

"I'm not going alone."

A waiter took my glass away.

"I'd like to come."

"Then come."

"It'll piss them off, Andie."

"Don't care. It's only for a few days. I can do this but I need you with me."

"Ok."

"Can you bring Rom?"

Seth scuffed his chin with the back of his hand. "Yeah." He nodded. "Let me see if I can swing it with Melissa."

I met Melissa twice. Didn't like her the first time. The second time, torture. She's as ambitious as she is self-serving. She took Rom away from Seth when the boy was two years old because she said her son needed a good role model of a father. Shit. A child needs a father to love him. An autistic child needs more than a parent. What Melissa wanted was a man to pamper her rich-bitch ambitions.

"How's Mac?"

"Not sure. Haven't talked to him much. Kate says the construction industry is slow. He doesn't need the work or the money."

"And Kate?"

"They've asked her to be a partner in the firm."

"Wow. You proud of her?"

"I suppose."

"She's sacrificed a lot to get this far. What does Mac think?"

"He doesn't know."

Seth roared.

"She's going to ask for a divorce."

"What?"

"Don't think she'll do it."

"When?" He sipped.

"Don't know."

I watched another couple sitting across from us. She laughed at something he said. He reached out and covered his hand with hers. I looked at Seth. He was watching them too.

"How's life as a part-time chef?"

He tried to smile. "Good, I guess. The manager says he wants me to start working with Astrid our head chef to help prepare menus for the fall and winter seasons."

"You'd like that?"

"I would. Something different."

"It's a big promotion."

"I really don't care what you think."

"Of course you do."

He placed his beer on the table. "I'm doing just fine, thanks."

"It's a long way from running your own restaurant."

"I'm a patient man."

"So patient your ex couldn't wait any longer for you to find yourself."

"I thought you said you wanted to have fun tonight."

"I enjoy it when I'm mocking you."

"And you know I let you just to give you a sense of purpose."

We raised our drinks and clinked them together. Seth ordered a burger and fries. He texted Melissa. She responded, giving him shit for asking about Tofino. I checked my phone, a half dozen ridiculous messages from students about assignments due next week. I would remind everyone tomorrow about due dates.

I glanced at Seth. "Still texting?"

He continued tapping.

I helped myself to a few fries. "Press her about Rom coming to Tofino."

He shook his head.

"What did she say?"

"She's being a bitch. Wants the details."

He continued tapping. Seth never stopped trying to placate his ex. He knew he'd never succeed, but that was Seth. He never gave up.

I polished off another glass. Inebriation ran through me like a transfusion.

THE ABSURDITY OF IT ALL

When Seth put his phone down he looked at me with those altruistic, warm blue eyes. Poor boy. I don't know what he saw in me.

"Feeling better?" he asked.

"Maybe. What's it to you?"

"A lot, if you want to know."

"It might come as a surprise Seth, I'm comfortable with me. What's wrong with me being self-serving? As a man, people would admire me."

"You think so?"

I plucked another fry from the plate. "I know so." And another fry. "I'm proud to be distanced, unengaged, unmotivated."

"You're establishing the mold of the modern Canadian woman."

"Doesn't work. Sarcasm isn't your thing. And Kate might not know it but her cold ambitions helped pave the way for my choices."

"It's easy to blame others."

"I'm not blaming her. I'm giving her credit."

He glanced at his phone.

I'm six years older than him. The professor and the student, that's how we first met. He proved to be the more astute political mind. I admired his passion. He fiercely believes what I used to—apathetic Canadians deserve the dysfunctional governments they've elected in the last twenty years. Seth hopes for a soapbox in radio. I have no inclinations to ignite fires under my students.

I have no inclination for anything, except reading. When I was twelve I lost myself in the reality of fiction. Up in my room with Charlie, my retriever, and Beth my best friend until she moved away, I read everything I could get my hands on. Dickens is compelling. There's vitality in bleak characters. They know how to survive. Hemmingway sucks. Oh, there's music in his sentences. Maybe I prefer authors like Stevenson and Maugham. Tolstoy can tell a story. I don't like funny, never liked Mowat. Munroe is depressing so she's worth reading. There's Edmund Morris, South African born, came to America a few years ago, he's a great biographer—hate his politics but love how he loves words. But Alice was, no, *Alice in Wonderland* is my favourite. It's the absurdity of it all.

Beth didn't think of me as a weirdo. She liked me because of my differences. She read my deeply distressing teenage angst poems. She liked to draw and imagine. We could be alone for hours and rarely utter a word. We never talked about our freakish ways.

She introduced me to late night clandestine sorties inside libraries around town. What times we had sneaking into the provincial legislative library late on a Friday night or conning ourselves past security into the vaulted chamber of dusty and faded tomes on the naval base in Esquimalt.

I grabbed the last two fries.

Seth put his glass down. "Do you know the painting by a guy, I think his name is Edvard Munch? I think he's Swedish."

"Norwegian."

"Norwegian?"

"Yes. And, you're probably thinking of *The Scream*. That's the name of the painting."

"Yeah."

"And?"

"I think the person in the painting is dying."

"What the hell are you doing on the phone?"

"I told you, texting with Melissa."

"Jesus, Seth. She brings out the strangest things in you."

"It's not her. I've been thinking about the painting for the last few days."

"You need a life. You need a real job and you need to write your book."

"I don't want to write a book."

"Yes, you do. Write the book and your radio gig will follow."

He ignored me. "Did you know Munch painted the image after walking one night he saw the sky turn blood red and he felt an infinite scream pass through nature?"

"You've been reading about him."

"Sometimes when I'm alone I feel an anguish so deep it has to be more than inside me."

"You mean your melancholy?"

"Melancholy's different. This anguish is a piercing sword running deep."

"As if you're dying?"

"As if I'm bearing the agony of every soul on earth."

I emptied my glass.

"Are you afraid of dying?" he asked.

"Why should I be? I don't have any plans to die soon. Even if I was dying I'm not sure I'd be afraid."

"Why?"

"If I'm dying there's nothing I can do."

"You'd just accept it?"

"Wouldn't you?" Our waiter passed by. I ordered another. "Actually, it's a stupid question."

"I don't think so."

"I do. But I like the painting. The shades of orange in the painting are variations of sunsets here in early winter."

"I'm afraid of dying."

"Oh Jesus, of course you are."

"Not because of me."

"Sure, Seth."

"Because of Rom. Because I don't know what would happen to him if I wasn't here."

Something stirred inside.

He noticed.

I didn't know what to say. Rom is the perfect child. Unlike me, he runs with the day. He means everything to his father.

Seth knew he had my attention. "And if Rom… I couldn't live without him. His interpretations of this crazy world keep me grounded. He sees things we don't."

A glass of wine arrived.

Seth continued. "He's oblivious to pride, greed, cruelty, the banality of life and along the way he's taught you a few lessons."

"Yeah." The buzz made it harder to think.

He sat up. "Jaymie texted me a while ago."

"What? What did she want?"

"She and John want us to come over Saturday."

"Why?"

"She wants me to make something for them, said I should come early and prep so everyone can see how it's done."

"You sure she doesn't have other motives?"

"She's married. And you've had too much to drink."

I felt foolish. "What are you going to make?"

"I don't know. Maybe I should make a crisp corn tortilla tapas."

"Sounds delicious."

"I would top it with sauteed cod, red onions, cilantro and pineapple and oyster tapas with pesto and melted parmesan cheese."

"You have to make chicken tapas."

"I will."

"When did they get back?"

"Monday. She said Paris was easy to navigate with all the locals on vacation. She said you and I should go."

I laughed. "You and me in Paris? Not a chance."

"I'd like to go."

"I'm not interested."

"I thought you said you wanted to go to Italy."

"I did. Not Paris."

"Why?"

"Prefer northern Italy. Fewer people. Better food. Less pretentious."

"I want to visit museums, study the Mona Lisa up close." He paused. "I'd like to go to restaurants, maybe not in Paris, but in Bordeaux."

"Don't be a friggin' snob."

"The Calabash stretches out along the backstreets of Bordeaux. The food is Caribbean. And speaking of tapas, they serve tapas individually or in group dishes. I've heard the Barbadian meatballs bathed in a coconut-curry sauce is maddening it is so good."

I emptied my glass.

He stood up. "Time to take you home."

"You can't stay tonight."

He hoisted me up, his arm around my waist. "You need to get some sleep."

TRUST

Rom's autism spectrum disorder causes him to obsess on the sounds of words. To him, haunting cadences, the highs and lows of pitch, the endless variations of the human voice hold his mind hostage. In the right circumstance, maybe the hush of a library, a single voice in the chaos of a school yard recess or the reverberations inside a near empty hockey arena, the human voice pulls him in.

And when he is listening you don't interrupt. Try to absorb as much as he does.

Afterwards, he might ask a few questions but more likely he will let the words sink in. And then, a few days, a few weeks later, he will ask something about what he heard. I'll remember too and try to answer him before Rom's mind races on to the next and the next. I've never been able to keep up. I'm not sure I want to. It's the journey he takes me on, I never know where we're going.

He's enthralled by audiobooks, including many of the stories I read as I child. With printed books, Rom can't read more than a few sentences before he's unable to retain the chain of events. He takes in more with audiobooks and listens to them over and over, never growing tired, each time picking out new elements, each time living the story as if it were his first experience.

On Sunday afternoon, he sat beside me listening to *Treasure Island*, the adventure of young Jim Hawkins. The narrators were superb. Today as the audio version unfolded it brought back memories of a summer long ago when I read about Long John Silver's mutinous efforts.

My swing glided lazily as I turned page after page in the hot morning sun. Shifting my ball cap lower to cover my eyes I adjusted my bottom on the hard, wooden seat. Suddenly out of the corner of my eye something moved. My eyes darted to the hedge. I didn't see anything in the shadows. And then a large body moved—an adult silver-tipped German shepherd sniffed the underbrush.

When he saw me his back stiffened. A low, angry snarl curled the lip revealing yellow menacing teeth. He shifted his head and torso towards me and growled.

I froze. Cold fingers clenched the ropes—the book slipped from my lap into the dirt. The shepherd's back bristled. He took a half-step. Jaws snapped. Another half-step. Yellow teeth and angry tangerine eyes forced me to look away. I felt him lunge, thudding to a stop a few feet in front of me. Coiled, shoulders humped, a growl thundered inside his chest.

And then a rock struck the dog on his flank. He yelped. Another rock, thrown from the yard next door landed at the shepherd's feet. He recoiled and barked, this time out of fear. A man's voice shouted. A rock stung the dog's ribs. His tail dropped as he sidestepped another missile. I craned my neck towards the fence but I didn't see anyone. I looked back to see the dog sprinting around the side of the house and out of view.

I waited, I'm not sure how long, and when I thought it safe I slipped off the swing and peered over the fence. The yard was empty.

That night I was reading in bed when Kate came to my room. I told her about the dog. I told her everything. She said she would thank the neighbour in the morning. Before she turned out the light she asked me if I was scared.

She sat on the bed.

"Andie, it's okay to be scared."

"Do you ever think about *Shelter-lady*?

"Why? she asked.

"*Shelter-lady* was scared."

"You're safe and *Shelter-lady* is too."

The next evening at dinner Kate told me she spoke to the neighbour's wife who said her husband was out at sea with the navy so it couldn't have been him who chased the dog away. The neighbour said she was home all day and never heard a dog barking. Kate asked me about the dog. I repeated my story. She spied Treasure Island and picked it up. She read for a while and then stopped. She smiled. She said she understood my story. Propping the book in her lap she read.

"*The captain spun round on his heel and fronted us; all the brown had gone out of his face, and even his nose was blue; he had the look of a man who sees a ghost, or the evil one, or something worse, if anything can be; and upon my word, I felt sorry to see him all in a moment turn so old and sick.*

'*Come, Bill, you know me; you know an old shipmate, Bill, surely,*' *said the stranger.*

The captain made a sort of gasp.

'*Black Dog!*' *said he.*

'*And who else? Returned the other, getting more at his ease. 'Black Dog as ever was, come for to see his old shipmate Billy, at the Admiral Benbow Inn.*"

Kate folded the book in her lap.

"I appreciate that you like to read but I wonder if you have imagined the German shepherd. A book like Treasure Island can cause a child to imagine things like dogs coming to life. Maybe it would be better if I took the book away for now. It might ease your mind.

"No, Mom. I want to read about Jim and Long John Silver. I didn't make up the story—there was a German shephard and he scared me and a man threw rocks and the dog ran away."

"I wonder if you are reading too much."

I started to cry.

She wilted and placed the book on the table.

"Andie, I want you to read only when I'm home, ok?"

"Ok."

"And if you are ever scared I will come and sit with you."

That summer before I turned into a cynical, self-hating teen, Kate and I spent a lot of time together. We took the ferry to Mayne Island where we stayed in a cottage down at the water overlooking the straight. Mac joined us for the last few days. Ferry boats pushed by every hour. We hiked the mountain in the centre of the island and at night baked salmon over an open fire. Idyllic as it was, I didn't know if I should happy so I pushed joy aside just in case those thoughts might cause Mac or Kate to leave again.

A few days before school I asked if we could hike the Sooke Hills. Mac overheard and said he would join us. On a cool August afternoon under slate skies we walked along abandoned logging roads, climbed steep slopes that overlooked Juan De Fuca Straight and waded through fields of fireweed where honey bees smothered the blossoms in one of the final dances of the season.

On our way back the three of us trudged downhill along a dusty abandoned road. It started to rain and it wasn't long before our shoes were caked in mud. When the road flattened out we stopped to catch our breath.

Mac scraped mud off his shoes on sharp rock poking out of the ground. "Did you hear about the German shepherd that's been wandering the neighbourhood?" he asked.

Kate stunned, looked at me then to Mac. "What do you mean?"

We were off again.

"Apparently, there's a shepherd roaming in and out of yards in our neighborhood. A few people have seen it. Bob Macklin, the guy who has bees, he told me he saw the dog. Fierce animal, he said. When Bob tried to chase the dog away the dog charged. He had to shield himself with a shovel. He tried striking the shepherd but he missed and the dog ran off."

Kate looked incredulous. "I don't believe it."

"Why not?"

She told him about my encounter with the shepherd.

Mac looked at me, his brow furrowed. "When did this happen?"

"I don't know, a few weeks ago."

"Probably the same dog." He rested his hand on my shoulder. "You were a brave girl. I'm impressed."

Kate's face was white. By the time we reached the car she hadn't said a word. It wasn't until we were past Sooke that she turned around. Her head shook. "I'm sorry, Andie. I'm sorry. I should have believed you."

ROM

Rom clicked the button and the audio book stopped. He rested a warm hand on my knee. "Andie, do you like Treasure Island?"

"I do. I read the book when I was your age."

"I like Cap'n Silver because he is very brave." He hopped off the couch and made his way to an ancient RCA Victor desktop radio where he turned on *The World at Six*.

Seth, standing in the kitchen, gestured with a hand clutching a tea towel. "Watch."

Rom settled cross-legged in front of the radio. He waited and when the broadcast began his oval brown eyes widened. He seldom blinked, sitting Buddha-like, occasionally glancing Seth's way, he made sure his father was nearby.

"He's taking it all in," I said.

"One day last week, he wouldn't stop talking after the broadcast. A woman read the news and Rom obsessed with her rhythms, her locution. The nuance of her voice, so different from the regular reader, he was so enthralled that when I tucked him in I sat for another twenty minutes just to calm him down."

"You have to wonder what is going inside his amazing brain."

Seth chuckled. "I'm not sure I want to know."

He slid a roast from the oven and lifted it onto a carving plate.

"What do the doctors say?" I dried off a serving bowl with a thick, white towel.

"Some autistic children enjoy numbers. Others music. Some have incredible aptitudes to draw and paint. There's a teenager in Vancouver who plays pinball video games. He's amongst the best in the world. Rom can't enough of words with compelling tempos."

"And the *World at Six?*"

"The narrator? The tempo of the script? I'm not sure."

"Does he like it as much as the beach?"

"Hard to say. On a windy day it's difficult to get him back in the car."

"Let's go after dinner."

"Ask him."

"After the news."

"Remember last time?"

I did. "He stood by the grove of trees above the water. He told us he was listening to the singing branches."

"Yeah, yeah. He had that faraway look in his eyes."

We headed to the beach after dinner. As soon as I parked my truck Rom opened the door and sprinted across the field until he reached the metal barrier overlooking the ocean. Raising both hands above his head, his fingers spread wide as the cool evening air rushed through. His curly locks flew off his forehead. We heard his gleeful shouts here at the street.

We followed as he navigated the stairs to the restless waters below.

At the water's edge, he turned into the incoming winds, his hands thrust out in front as he attempted to catch the gusts. Then clutching his hands around the air, he raised both fists above him before slowly unlocking his fingers. He did this over and over until a gust smacked full on and Rom teetered uneasily.

We raced to him.

His hands fell to his side to help regain balance.

I zipped my jacket to my chin. "It's cold."

Rom turned to us. "My ears are windy."

I laughed. "Mine too."

He pointed to the sky where squawking seagulls floated overhead. "Look."

"What?"

"Seagulls are falling."

"They're floating. They won't fall."

He began to flap his arms in encouragement. "Flap your wings. Flap your wings."

I copied him. "Seagulls, don't fall, okay?"

"They're not very smart, Andie."

Just then another large gust struck. We craned our necks as the gulls drifted inland.

"Watch me, Andie." He edged nearer the water as a surging wave caught him ankle deep.

"Water! Water, Daddy." He chirped, "Cap'n Silver has salty sea legs. See. See. Cap'n Silver on a peg leg."

He tried standing on one leg but faltered.

Seth stepped forward just as another wave swept around them.

"Wet, Daddy."

"Do you want to come out?"

"No, Daddy. Cap'n Silver has salty sea legs." His right leg began to sink into soft sand. "Cap'n Silver's peg—."

He tottered. Seth grabbed his shoulders, pulling the boy out as another wave crashed around them.

"Time to come out of the water Cap'n."

"No. No… Cap'n Silver wants to stay in the sea, Daddy."

"But the water's cold." He took Rom's hand.

"No Daddy. I want to listen to the sea."

"You can listen with us. Here, hold Andie's hand."

I clasped his freezing hand in mine. "Cap'n, it's better to stay ashore," I said.

"Cap'n Silver is cold, Andie."

"Do you want to go back to the truck?" I asked.

He shook his head. "I'm listening to the winds. It is very noisy don't you think?"

Seth beamed.

Rom's hand stretched out again and again grasping at the wind. A blast pushed him back. He laughed. His pants were soaked to his knees. He was shivering but he didn't care.

I glanced at Seth. Christ, how I envied him.

"Cap'n, it's cold. You're shivering."

"I'm cold, Daddy."

"We should go home, son."

"I'm having fun. Don't you think it's important to have fun?"

"More than anything, my boy. But we can come back again, okay?"

We started up the stairs.

"You can come too, Andie."

"Next time I want to catch the wind like you, Rom."

"It's really not hard. But I can show you if you like."

"I'd like that very much."

As we approached the truck Rom asked, "Can Andie sit with me in the back?"

"Yes, if that's what you would like."

He was still shivering as we settled into the truck. I wrapped my coat around his legs. Seth started the truck and turned on the heat.

"Are you cold, Andie?"

"No, Cap'n Silver."

"Cap'n Silver almost fell in."

"Did you have a good time?"

"I did. I really, did because you came with us. I want you to come again, Andie. Please will you come again?"

"Of course. But next time Cap'n Silver should stay out of the water."

He nodded triumphantly, leaned his body against mine and looked up, "Can we come back tomorrow?"

TAPAS

As I stepped into Jaymie's kitchen, Seth busied himself pinching off prawn tails, surrounded by a colourful array of ingredients laid out tidily, all within easy reach. He was happy.

"Am I too late for the impressive cooking show?" I dropped my purse on the counter.

He pulled another tail off a prawn. "Not at all, just getting set up. Where were you?"

I held up a bottle of wine. "This." I looked around. "Where are our hosts?"

"Jaymie's at the store picking up baguettes. John's at work, should be home soon."

Just then Jaymie came through the back door with a bag of groceries in one hand and a cat under her arm. She dropped the cat on the floor where it scurried to safety down the hallway.

She was my only girlfriend.

"Andie! When did you get here?"

"Just now."

She wrapped her arms around me and kissed me on the cheek. "You look good," she said.

"And Paris?"

"You have to go. You really do."

I looked at Seth. He tried to hide a snigger.

She reached in to the bag and began hauling groceries out placing the various items on the counter.

She looked great. Short and petite with dark hair in a ponytail, Jaymie, always running or at yoga, packed more energy in her body than four women. Her spirit, as inquisitive as a child, reminded me of Seth who thought Jaymie's curiosity about the possibilities of life made her an ideal mother. She found my indifference amusing. "Who does that?" she asked Seth at Christmas last year.

She never judged me.

Where are the kids?" I asked.

"At John's parents. They cherish having the kids over a few days a month."

"Don't you miss them?"

"Every second."

"And texting drives them mad?"

She laughed. "How did you know?"

"Seth does it too. Drives me crazy."

He ignored us.

A necklace of typewriter keys jingled around Jaymie's neck. When she moved to the fridge her energetic steps caused the keys to twist in rhythmic dances that mirrored her personality. Innocent and unscarred, she lived an ideal life, if you like predictability. It's not so much Jaymie but John who insists upon planning and purpose and everything in its place. Jesus, the drapes hang perfectly straight, the floors gleam and even a master gardener ensures the house looks ideal from the street.

Jaymie poured herself a glass of sparkling water. I watched her bring the glass to her lips. Her eyes were on Seth.

"I admire you," she said.

He continued de-tailing prawns. "Why?"

"Because you're creating and you're energized."

"A new dish excites me. There are so many options in what I ultimately create."

Her head bobbed. Her hand waved at the colourful aromatic spread. "You're creating a banquet, not cooking dinner. It's obvious."

I snorted. "You are talking about Seth."

"I like to see what's in front of me, take it all in. When I start to work all the ingredients are at play. You have to let the possibilities simmer in your mind before you begin."

"Let the possibilities simmer. I like it."

"Oh, Jesus. Will you two shut up."

Seth winked at Jaymie before dropping a handful of prawns into a bowl of cold water. He wiped his hands on a towel.

She snatched a prawn and peeled it. "You don't mind if I assist?"

"Of course not. We'll leave Andie to supervise."

As Jaymie peeled prawns Seth went to the fridge and pulled out a bag of mussels spilling them into the sink.

The front door opened, a boisterous voice hollered, "Anybody home?"

"We're in the kitchen," Jaymie chirped.

John stepped into the room. Behind him a thick, thunderous man filled the doorway.

"What's going on here?" John inquired. He moved around the island next to Seth. "Smells damn good. What is it?"

"Tapas in decadent arrays as per Jaymie's instructions. How are you, John?"

"Fine, just fine, Seth." John swiveled around and gestured towards the man behind him. "This is Andie and Seth, good friends of Jaymie's."

The man ignored me. He waved half-heartedly towards Seth.

"Andie and Seth, this Brent Jennings."

I waved back in jest.

The asshole ignored me. Instead, his eyes were on Jaymie.

"Hey, beautiful." John pulled her tight and kissed her on the cheek. "Missed you today."

"How's the store?" she asked.

"Tell you later. I should get this guy settled in first."

Jaymie's eyes flickered resentment.

He gestured to Brent. "Let's head up."

Brent moved past me into the hallway.

Shit. It's like I'm not even in the room.

Half way down the hallway John bellowed, "Beers are in the fridge, Seth. Help yourself."

As soon as they were out of range I asked, "Who the hell is he? Jesus!"

"He's an old friend of John's." Her head shook. "I didn't know he was in town and I'm pissed John would spring him on us."

"What does he do?"

"Brent's a consultant for the oil industry."

"Oh shit." I laughed.

"What?" Jaymie sliced a baguette.

"A right-wing conservative from the oil patch? Should be an interesting night."

"Seth!" Jaymie cried out as a baguette flew across the island towards him.

He stabbed at the loaf and sent it crashing to the floor. "What are you doing?"

She snickered. "I'm trying to help."

I sipped as both continued working head down, neither saw the silly smile on the face of the other.

Seth warmed olive oil in a sauté pan over medium heat. He added garlic and red pepper flakes, sautéing ever so briefly. "It's critical I don't burn the garlic." Turning the gas lower he added the shrimp, lemon juice, sherry and paprika, stirring briskly until the shrimp turned pink and began to curl. When the shrimp was ready he transferred the dish to a warm plate. Jaymie placed the baguettes into the broiler.

The enticing aromas pushed aside niggling doubts and the buzz from the wine soothed. This was Seth's night. He was preparing a great meal. I wasn't going to screw this up for him. *It shouldn't be hard to stay out Brent's line of sight.*

Jaymie plucked a prawn from a plate and bit into it. "Oh, my God. Let's have our own party!"

Seth tried to assure me, "You and Brent are going to hit it off just fine."

"I'm going to be on my best behaviour."

Jaymie snatched another prawn. "Brent can be a little overbearing. Best to humour him."

KEYS OF HOPE

"I hope everyone is hungry." Jaymie gushed.

Seth sat next to me, pleased with his work. Everyone was seated.

John was ebullient, "Seth, this looks absolutely decadent." "Thank you, you've outdone yourself." He raised a glass and we toasted Seth and the meal.

Brent began to chat with John as if they were the only ones in the room. I glanced at Jaymie. Her eyes narrowed.

Behind her, I spotted two framed pictures of her children—a daughter with fire in her eyes, ready to take on the world, and a handsome young man shy in front of the camera. I glanced at John. He was a good businessman. A good father? I had no reason to think otherwise.

My gaze returned to the table. Brent eyed me, ready to pounce. I took the plate of mussels from Jaymie and served myself just as John teased out a playful question for Brent. "Are you in covert disguise this trip?"

This prick was all bravado. Stocky and big boned, only casual slacks and an open short-sleeved shirt softened his presence. His wary green-grey eyes surveyed the room as if he expected to find something he didn't like.

He looked me over.

"Found something you like?"

His eyes darted away.

Jaymie's faced reddened.

John attempted to move us on. "Brent's consulting work tends to draw the wrath of many in this province."

Seth nodded politely.

"You're here for important meetings, are you?" I couldn't resist a pinch of sarcasm.

He responded to John. "I have meetings with two First Nations leaders in the morning and staff from the premier's office in the afternoon."

The room went quiet. I filled my glass. *I'm not letting Seth down. This guy is an ass but I'm not playing his game.*

Brent went on the attack. "I wonder what a political scientist like you thinks of the pro-business approach of government."

"Really?" I asked.

"Really."

"As a political scientist I don't have an opinion. A pro-business approach, particularly for a resource-based province like Alberta dependent on digging holes in the ground, that's the prerogative of elected officials. If you want a political opinion you should ask Seth. He's the political mind you want to debate."

Seth laughed and shook his head. "Not now. Not tonight."

The conversation gained momentum. Brent continued glancing my way. I avoided contact by weighing in on family and vacations. And then John took over. Enthused by the ins and outs of the travel business, he explained the need to reinvent packages for customers in a competitive market. He talked about exchange rates and the importance of planning a vacation well in advance of the departure date.

Jaymie tried to jump in but John, keen to get his point points across, breezed on. It was almost as if he was trying to impress Brent.

She caught me studying her. Oh, Jesus. She couldn't hide her anger.

Seth interrupted the tedium. "Brent, did I hear earlier that you have two boys?"

"I do."

"How old?"

"Ten and eight."

"My son's ten. And your sons play hockey?"

"Definitely."

"Do you coach them?

"No. I'm far too busy to have the time to commit."

"That's too bad, isn't it?"

"I suppose."

"Children their ages are so full of promise. To coach them is to open the world to its possibilities."

Brent straightened himself in the chair.

Seth picked up steam. "I'd coach my son but he doesn't play team sports. They aren't quite his thing."

"Too bad," Brent offered. "Team sports build character."

"I agree."

Brent scanned the room. He stopped at me. "I expect my boys to learn dedication and the benefits of hard work and sacrifice."

Seth wasn't to be denied. "That doesn't sound like play, it sounds like work."

"Seth's son has incredible aptitudes for interpreting the many variations of the human voice," I said.

Shithead ignored me. "Seth, play is fine. I'm all for children enjoying themselves but my boys need to learn important lessons of life."

"Such as empathy?"

"Empathy? That's asking a lot of children."

"I've witnessed it with Rom on the soccer field."

"My boys don't play soccer. The game's too soft."

Seth looked around the table. "Do you mind if I share a story?"

Jaymie saw a way forward. "Please, Seth."

Trust Seth. He stepped in front of me and I was grateful. *This was going to be fun.*

"Rom is in most ways a typical ten-year-old boy. He's curious about everything, he asks questions whenever he sees something he doesn't understand and like most boys his age he's awkward around girls. Not long ago I went to see him play soccer one afternoon after school.

"I arrived late and as I stepped out of the car I heard screams and shouts of children running across the field. The game was frenetic, chaos prevailed. I found my place among the parents and looked for my son across the field where the coaches implored the kids to pass the ball. I thought Rom would be watching from the sidelines.

"But he was on the field where a tightly packed jumble of kids chased the ball. Rom, easy to spot, stood a good distance from the others, watching the game unfold. His steps were tentative. When the ball came his way and the children shouted, he froze, his arms raised in defence, his body now sideways to avoid interaction. The ball rolled by, the swarm of boys and girls whooshed excitedly in pursuit. Rom's arms dropped and the biggest smile crossed his face. He chased the pack."

I looked around the table. Brent listened politely. Jaymie and John were trapped inside the story. Jaymie's knife and fork rested on the plate. She sat back, tilting her head to catch every word.

Seth continued.

"Rom doesn't run well and when someone kicked the ball downfield he fell behind the others. He slowed and reverted again to watching the game unfold from a distance. Occasionally, one of his teammates would shout to him, encouraging Rom to join the game. He tried. He couldn't stay with them. But this was big for Rom. He took it all in.

"Unfortunately, too much stimuli soon tired him and he walked off the field. The coach substituted a new player. Rom was anxious."

"Why?" Jaymie asked.

"He wanted to be a part of it like the others but the excitement, the shouting and the outbursts," Seth's hands gestured caution, "sometimes it's too much. Even with him on the sidelines I knew the excitement still bubbled up inside. If he's unable to find a release he shuts himself off. He turned his back to the field. His hands covered his ears.

"Coach Cheryl came to him. She's a great teacher. He trusts her unconditionally. She tried to calm him, tried to bring him back before he withdrew inside himself."

Brent's eyes narrowed.

"Cheryl's hand rested softly on Rom's back, her head nodded slowly next to his. And then, he turned to the field and ran out.

"The game was almost over and the ball moved across the field towards Rom's goal net. He teetered on the edge of the scrum. One of his teammates came out and took his hand. He resisted at first, but slowly the two immersed themselves inside the pack. There must have been fifteen players around the ball and suddenly the ball tumbled out and rolled right to Rom.

"Everyone stopped. All eyes were on my son. They waited. Players on both teams encouraged him and as shouts from the children grew louder Rom raised a leg and stopped. He tightened up. Patience is the best recourse with him but out there on the field everyone waited for my son to kick the ball."

Seth paused. "There's one more thing you should know. Rom doesn't understand the game. He knows there are teams but he doesn't understand the objective of one team winning over the other. Scoring goals, yes. He doesn't distinguish between one net belonging to his team and one belonging to the other.

"So, when he finally kicked the ball, and he kicked it hard, he kicked it right into his own goal. His hands shot above his head. He dashed into the net and wrapped both arms around the ball, clutching it tight to his chest. Even from the sidelines I heard him shout, 'Goal! Goal!'

"A teammate cheered. Someone on the other team clapped and then players from both teams joined the celebration. It was entirely spontaneous."

Seth glared at Brent. "Everyone understood."

He turned to me and beamed. "That's what I call empathy."

Jaymie clapped her hands. "Bravo. Bravo. Great story. Thank you, Seth." She looked around. "Anyone for dessert?"

Exasperation popped crimson pigments across Brent's cheeks.

As she skipped into the kitchen the keys around Jaymie's neck jingled a hint of elation, punctuating Seth's narrative.

PROMISES, PROMISES

Seth sat back on the chaise lounge on my deck. "Do we ever know what we want?"

"Ah, the philosopher."

"I'm serious."

"I'm sure you are."

"I wonder if I've let you down."

Ignore him.

"I wonder if I could be a better role model."

"You think I need a role model?"

"If I didn't play your games of ridicule maybe things would be better."

"You're kidding?"

"I'm not. I wonder if I play along too often."

"You think I'd be a better person if I didn't mock you?"

"If I didn't play along."

"Jesus, Seth."

"I'm not sure about us."

"And so am I when you talk like this."

He sat up and faced me sideways, dropping his feet onto the deck. "Last week wasn't an argument. We fought because you were drunk and you didn't even know it."

"What the hell are you talking about?"

"You know."

"I really don't."

"I shouldn't drink with you anymore."

"Stop questioning yourself."

"Maybe I encourage you to drink."

I finished the wine in my glass. "Do you know how ridiculous you sound?"

"What if I don't drink with you and your drinking stops?"

"Tell you what, come with me to the pub. Don't drink. Let's see if that helps."

"Don't laugh. I want to help."

Help what? You think I need help?"

His voice rose. "This isn't working. Us, it isn't working."

I shrugged. "All we do is hang out. How is this not working?"

"I want us to—"

"You're under an illusion our hanging out matters more."

"And you don't?"

I laughed hard.

"It's not funny."

"If you think we have a relationship—"

"We *do* have a relationship."

"Oh, Seth. First you tell me I drink too much. Now you're concerned about our relationship."

"You're a bitch."

"Poor boy. Another myth shattered."

"What you did last week… It was wrong, Andie."

"What do you mean?"

"You can't show up drunk in a hospital."

"Did I do that or did you imagine it?"

"You were drunk. You pushed a security guard."

"I don't think so."

"You don't remember screaming and calling him an asshole?"

I looked past Seth into the harbour.

He barked, "You don't remember, do you? You staggered into Emergency shouting Rom's name until security stopped you."

"I didn't do—"

"It gets worse. When I came out of Rom's room you were in the grasp of security, two guys—you were punching and kicking and when I tried to intervene, you didn't recognize me—you didn't even know me."

"I... don't remember."

"Christ, Andie. Rom was in emergency. We didn't know if he had suffered a seizure."

He shook with anger. "When I saw you, my first reaction was to make sure Rom was safe from you."

I couldn't look at him.

"You're in deep. You're in deep and I don't know how to help you."

"You think because someone shows up in a public place a little over indulged she has a problem? Does it make you feel superior? Does it?"

"I'm trying to—"

"Fuck you! Don't..." My voice screeched to a whisper. "Don't ever tell me what to do."

"I'm the one who should be angry."

"You call me a drunk and you had me kicked out of the hospital but oh yeah, you're the one who should be mad? You make me tired Seth. You know what...?"

I brushed by him into the condo, yanked a wineglass from the cabinet and grabbed a bottle. I poured until wine rimmed the top. "Fuck you, Seth McCallister!"

He charged into the room.

I gulped at the wine until the glass was empty and threw it against the fireplace where it smashed as splinters spilled across the floor.

"What the hell are you doing?"

I grabbed another and filled it, gulping again and again until Seth grabbled me from behind. I struggled, twisting in his arms. The glass slipped from my hands. I watched it fall spilling merlot until it exploded on the hardwood floor. A sharp pain stabbed my right foot. Thick, dark blood mixed with the merlot.

I broke free. More shards pierced my feet as I reached for the cabinet. I was pouring another when Seth yanked me away, punching the glass from my hand, sending the glass across the room.

His arms wrapped around me lifting me off the ground.

"Stop it! Stop this now."

He dragged me to the kitchen and laid me on the floor. I squirmed to get up.

He bawled. "Don't move. You're bleeding. Don't… move."

I struck at him, smacking him on the thigh. "You fucking bastard. Get out! Get out of my place. NOW!"

He ignored me.

Blood oozed from both feet.

"Don't. Move. You might have glass inside you." He pulled a chair over and rested both my feet on it. Blood pooled on the seat, dollops fell to the floor.

Grabbing a towel from the kitchen he gingerly dabbed the souls of my left foot.

I recoiled. "Christ!"

"I can see a piece inside. Do you have tweezers?"

"In the bathroom across from my bedroom."

When he came back he knelt on one knee and with a hand on my heel plucked at the broken shard. I squirmed. He clasped and yanked hard.

"Fuck."

"Let me check the other wounds." Dabbing, probing, he examined each cut pressing them wider to peer inside.

My fingers white-knuckled the chair.

"I have to make sure there's no glass inside you. Otherwise you're going to the hospital."

"Funny. Funny man. Weren't you the one who had me kicked out?"

He continued examining my wounds. "I don't see any glass. Just these." He dropped a halo stained sliver next to the others.

"Those were inside me?"

"Felt pretty good, I bet."

"Didn't feel it at all."

He tried to hide a smile. "Because you're heartless and numb to this world."

"Shut up."

"You're still bleeding. Keep your feet on the chair."

"How many cuts?"

"Five, three on this and two on your right foot."

Using the blood-soaked-towels he applied pressure until the wounds began to coagulate. Later, he pulled himself up and stood over me. "Leave those wrapped for now. I'm going to go wash my hands."

My limp body rested against the wall. My head slumped to my chest. As he came into the room I looked up as strands of hair fell across my face but not before I saw the desperation in his eyes.

He tried to smile. "You look like shit."

"Don't laugh."

"Do I look like I'm laughing?"

I tried to get up. "This hurts. Can I sit on a chair?"

He hoisted me from behind.

"Better?"

I closed my eyes.

"Andie…" He hesitated.

"What?"

"We can't do this."

I shrugged.

"You're a storm rolling into darkness."

"You'd like to think that."

"We should separate." His voiced cracked. "For a while."

I heard myself say, "Maybe we should."

"It's not that I want to—"

"Jesus, Seth. Not hanging out isn't going to change things. I've been an ass."

"Then what is?"

"I don't know. I don't know." I knew one thing. Seth was coming apart.

He moved to the deck as a seaplane revved its engines preparing for take-off. I twisted my body and peered outside. Above us dark, billowing clouds scudded low over purple mountains. Seth leaned against the railing.

Maybe we should separate for a while. I wanted to cry.

He looked back at me. Of course, he did. Those eyes. What am I supposed to do?

I crawled outside and rolled into the first available lounge.

"I told you to stay off your feet."

Can't look at him.

He waited.

I blurted out, "If you think there is a problem then I'm willing to consider your advice."

"What?"

"I'm going to trust you." I didn't know what I was saying. I didn't know what to say next.

He sat down on the side of the lounge.

"What if I don't drink while we're in Tofino?"

"Andie…"

"It's a start." I held out a hand.

He covered mine with his. "Yes, it is."

"Can we give it a shot?"

His eyes softened. "Can you do it?"

I looked away. "Of course."

He unwrapped the towels and surveyed the cuts.

"The bleeding has almost stopped." He rested my feet on a clean towel and continued inspecting the wounds. "Do I have to hang out with your parents for three days?"

"Yes, and so do I."

"Oh, Rom can't come."

"What?"

I couldn't hide my disappointment.

"He has a doctor's appointment on the Friday."

"You can't move the appointment?"

"The doctor wants to confirm medications will control possible seizures. Melissa insists we keep this date."

I closed my eyes. "But you will come. You're not abandoning me?"

"At great peril. If Rom needs meds Melissa will be a basket case."

"She already is. You being there wouldn't make a difference."

"I'm sorry Rom can't come."

"I wanted to take him hiking."

"Hiking?"

"You'll see."

Seth pointed to my feet. "I'll bandage them later. I'm going inside to clean up your mess."

"My mess?"

"Definitely yours."

A while later he came out on the deck and leaned on the railing. Dusk shrouded the city.

"You'll keep your promise?"

"Of course."

TOFINO

My unease for the weekend further soured on the drive up to the resort. Moody and my sarcastic best by the time we pulled into the resort, I had withdrawn. The last thing Seth wanted was stilted conversations with Mac and Kate, a mother and daughter at odds, while the cracks of divorce threatened to disintegrate all around us.

Nerves vibrated.

Poor Seth. He had no idea how dark his world was about to become. For now, he worried about Rom's appointment. After we checked in he called Melissa. His phone tucked between cheek and shoulder, freed his hands to haul our bags up to our room. He dropped the bags and continued talking, if talking described the back and forth jousting of old conflicts born again.

He paced. He swore under his breath. When the conversation ended, he threw the phone at the couch.

"What did the doctor say?"

"What?" He looked without seeing me.

"What did the doctor say?"

"The stupid bitch." He exhaled. And focused. "It's good news. He said there's no permanent damage from the seizure."

"Good then. Forget about the bitch."

He ran both hands through his thinning hair. "Christ."

"Feel better?"

"You have no idea. I kept thinking the worst as I drove up and how Melissa would hold it over me if the news was bad and I wasn't there. I'm exhausted."

"And you haven't even hung out with Mac and Kate."

"After Rom's news I can live with anything."

"What happens now?"

"The doctor is recommending medications for six months. Melissa, in her usual way, said no."

"What?"

"Her research says Rom's meds are all he needs."

"I didn't know she's a doctor?"

"I'm going to call the doctor when I get back. I want to hear from him."

"But Rom's going to be fine?"

"Yeah." He looked around the suite and exhaled. "Very nice." He carried my suitcase into the bedroom and dropped it on the bed.

"Are you ready for this?" he asked.

I shrugged. "I've seen variations of their dysfunction over the years. Now it's your turn to settle in on the calamity we call family."

"Can't wait."

We stood on the deck that overlooked Cox Bay. The tide was out and a setting sun glistened over wet compacted sand. Couples and families strolled as dogs chased sticks and below us a dozen or so men and women in wetsuits sat in on a surfing lesson.

Somewhere deep inside a warming relief made me shudder. I used to love this place.

"You like?" I asked.

He surveyed the crowds scattered across the beach. "I could stay here all day."

"Let's go for a walk."
"Now?"
"Yes."
"What about your parents?"
"We have time. We don't have to see them until eight."
Seth stretched.
"We won't go far. Promise." I grabbed a coat from my bag. "Put a sweater on."

As we came around the corner of the resort a cool wind buffeted. We scrambled to the beach along a path narrowing to a sandy trench moving single file past guests heading back to the resort. Ringlets of my hair whipped and bobbed in my face.

The bay stretched northwest and southeast and with the tide out the beach expanded so it was possible to wander here for hours. I tacked northwest into the wind. Seth pulled his sweater over his head.

"It's a little cool for September."
"Have you been here in November?"

We walked on the edge of a vast ocean. Out there, the magnificent Pacific ruled for several thousand miles. The wind on my face stung forcing pores to open and the stench of my wine-soaked body spilled out.

My paced quickened.
"Slow down."
I shook my head.
"Jaymie's wants me to give her cooking lessons."
"Of course she does. What kind?"
"I'm not sure. I think she liked the tapas I made last month."
"Let's head over there," I pointed.
"Where?"
"To those rocks. There's a path. We'll trek through the trees to an outcropping you can't see from here. It looks out to the sea."

I zipped my coat.

"Cold?"

"I'll be fine." My arms pistoned back and forth. "Do you like her?"

"Who?"

"Jaymie."

"She's nice, yeah."

"Do you find her attractive?"

"She's married, Andie."

"And marriage matters?"

We moved off the beach up a short path into the forest. The sun had already set behind the firs whistling high in the briny air.

"Do you find her attractive?"

"Andie, don't."

"It's a simple question."

The path turned left and began to drop. I plunged forward. "It's this way." We wound back and forth then dropped down to a small foot bridge.

"Yeah, she's pretty."

"Just your kind I think."

"Why are you doing this?"

"She's open to things. She's energetic. I know she likes you."

"As a friend."

"Perhaps."

Seth puffed. "She's been married eight years."

It was almost pitch black down here. I stopped. "After this bridge we head up through those trees."

"I see daylight."

"Almost there."

By now the boardwalk had disintegrated, replaced by damp earth and protruding rocks strewn amongst forearm thick tree-root knots forcing us to scavenge for the easiest way forward. We climbed straight before veering sharply left and then straight again.

Seth tugged on my sleeve. "Stop for a second." He pointed to a night sky where a few stars shimmered.

"Isn't it crazy?"

"What am I supposed to see?"

"Just watch."

More stars emerged.

"This is a window on the universe."

"You're telling me this because?"

"This tiny window has experienced more than all of human history."

"You don't know that."

"I like to imagine it."

"I know you do."

"Our eyes can only see so much, Andie. Our imaginations give us room to grow."

I turned to go.

"You're enjoying yourself? Out here, I mean," he asked.

"Yeah."

"I can feel it in your voice."

"Feel it?"

"You have Rom's enthusiasm."

"Maybe."

The path snaked back and forth, climbing over soft mossy undergrowth that soon gave way to broken shale.

"We're almost there."

"You keep saying that."

From here the sunset had faded to peach and plum.

I pointed. "Out here, more than anything, I'm free."

"What do you mean? Where are you going?"

"Come on." Around the outcropping the ground leveled out. Here and there tufts of grass peeked out from splintered rocks. Gusts tossed hair into my face. I stepped off the path and sat on a large boulder.

I was home.

Seth bent over catching his breath.

I glanced back to the beach. Below us a couple with two small children, a boy and a girl, ran ahead of their parents, their voices cascading across the sand. As the boy ran, his sister yelled for him to stop, stomping her bare feet in a shallow tidal pool. She laughed and stomped again. Water splashed her legs. Her brother noticed and turned back to join her. A game began, they jumped up and down trying to empty the water, each child striving to outdo the other. Their parents joined in. Laughing voices echoed.

I huddled from the wind behind Seth and looked out into eternity. "*This*, is why I came this weekend."

"Are you happy?"

"When I'm here I'm free from the darkness inside."

"Then we'll do this more often."

"In my teens I hiked by myself in the hills behind the resort. I never wanted to leave."

"I like seeing you this way."

"Don't get used to it."

"I wish… I wish we could be—"

"No, Seth. You wouldn't like me very much."

I pointed across the bay. "See how the shoreline curls against the hills over there?"

He searched.

I pointed to a bank of trees, dark clusters in the fading light, undulating for several hundred yards until the ridge wrapped itself into a lazy curl protecting a good part of the bay.

"We'll hike there tomorrow."

"*I wouldn't like you?* What do you mean?"

"Because I don't like myself. I'll ask the kitchen staff to pack a lunch for us." I glanced up at him. "I hope you're not disappointed."

"Of course I am."

I pointed across the bay. "When a westerly blows and we're under those trees the whistling branches make you feel as if you were inside a house."

"I'd build a house there."

"Ha. I've often thought it's an ideal location. It would have three levels with lots of windows, a vaulted cedar ceiling and a woodstove burning during winter months. See there, on the ridge, the views out to the Pacific are perfect while the lower levels of the house would be sheltered from the storms."

The wind whipped our faces and the burn on my cheeks stung. Tucking my knees under my chin, my arms encircled my legs.

Happy? Yeah. For now.

DIVORCE

On the deck of our suite we watched silhouettes cluster in disparate locations across the beach. Carefree voices echoed into our lives. Seth said nothing about my abstinence. Maybe he was afraid if he said something he'd tip the cart and I'd take a sip and it would be downhill from there. He was right, but out here I didn't want to think about withdrawals or tremors. Booze and this decaying mass, they're the same. "We should go," I said.

"I'd rather not."

"We'll stay until my parents make you shudder. Then we get out and walk the beach again. Okay?"

"I'm not looking forward to this."

"I need you tonight."

He put an arm around my waist. "I like it when you use those words."

I knocked on the door of Mac and Kate's suite, turned the doorknob and forced myself in.

Mac sat with his back to the door, his words bitter. "You never finish your sentences when you talk to me."

"Maybe it's because I know you're not listen—." Kate rose stiffly from her chair. A frozen smile erupted. "Andie. Come in. Come in, both of you." She moved around Mac and approached with arms extended. The embrace was all too brief.

Mac pulled himself out of the chair. "Hello, my daughter."

We hugged. He stepped back.

"Haven't seen you in months," I said.

"Now, now. You know I've been busy. But I've missed you."

"Not so much. You haven't called."

Kate's lukewarm voice trailed away. "Thank you for coming, Seth. I hope all is well."

"Yes, thank you."

He turned to Mac and they shook hands.

"Good to meet you again, Seth. I'm pleased you've joined us this weekend."

"Thank you, sir."

I sniggered.

Mac's big frame shuffled into the living room. "Come in. Come in. I thought we should have a glass of champagne before dinner."

The livingroom's three massive windows revealed a panorama of beach and ocean.

Seth and Mac moved to the main window.

"Magnificent view," Seth offered.

"We never get tired of this, do we, dear?"

Kate had moved into the kitchen. She didn't respond. A moment later she returned with a glass of white wine.

I rolled my eyes at Seth.

"How is the restaurant business?" Kate asked.

"It's good. Lots of tourists are in town this summer so business is brisk. The cruise ships are essential. I think we're doing well."

"Where do you work?"

"Covetus Auvergne on lower Yates. It's a new restaurant in an Old World charm brick building. We serve an eclectic mix of west coast favourites."

"I see." Kate stared past us looking for a way out.

"Please, please…" Mac's voice rumbled. "Find a seat." He gestured with his cigar hand. "The champagne should be ready."

I was surprised how much weight he'd gained. At six foot four his suit jacket hung open and a pale blue shirt gaped at his gut. His hair, still jet black and usually neat was unruly, curls wisped around the ears. I missed his smile.

Mac twirled the champagne in the ice bucket. "You any good?" He looked at Seth.

"Our customers think so. I love what I'm doing."

"If you have a passion for your work, you have a leg up on the competition. Take care of your customers and you have a future."

"Now," Mac brought up the bottle, "I think this is cold."

Kate's attention remained in Cox Bay.

"I'm not drinking this weekend."

Mac chortled. "What? Andie…" He poured champagne and handed the first glass to me. "You must have some of this."

I took the glass. Seth eyed me. I wanted the booze. I needed this. My hands trembled.

Mac poured three more. Seth took one and handed it to Kate who promptly placed the glass on the window sill. Mac raised his, brought his cigar to his mouth and puffed. The blue haze billowing into the ceiling made me think of the divorce.

He pulled himself up and moved to the middle of the room. "This may well be our last family trip. We've had many great times—"

Kate sighed. "Can't we do this without a sideshow?"

He gestured with the cigar to her. "All right." He nodded to Seth. "Thank you for coming with Andie. I'm not sure she would have come without you."

Seth hesitated.

Mac held his glass high, "Cheers to a civil weekend. May we focus on the good times, may we share some of our fondest memories."

I put my glass on the table. Kate grabbed the wineglass and stepped out on the balcony.

Mac couldn't hide the sadness. "It's been a big day for the both of us."

I wanted to go to her.

His empathy was palpable. "I'm sorry to see her like this. Kate's a good woman." His voice was as rueful as his words. "This is my fault."

"It was a long time ago, Mac."

He turned to Seth. "Andie learned to hike here. I don't think she remembers but her first with me occurred in the hills behind the resort."

Mac's eyes glistened. "You were six years old."

I patted the seat next to me and tucked my hands under my legs. Seth sat down.

Mac puffed. "You used to dawdle behind me. Even when you were older you dawdled. Do you remember?"

"I… I'm not sure."

"Do you remember the salamander?"

The memory flashed. "I do."

"We were on our way back from an afternoon hike. At one point, I turned around to see if you were with me. There you were, on your knees peering into the underbrush. You asked if I had ever seen a salamander."

"What did you say?" I asked.

"You don't remember? I told you we would find one."
"Did we?"
"Andie… You don't remember?"
I tried but couldn't.
"A while later we emerged from a clearing. I stopped. You were behind and bumped into me. On the path in front of us a salamander stood motionless. You spied it right away and pushed forward."

Suddenly the image of the salamander popped into my head—small, perfect, motionless.

Mac waved the cigar. "I crept on my knees." He spread his other hand in front. "I cupped this over the salamander and gathered it in." He chuckled. "You stepped back as I opened my hand but you were close enough to see the bright greens and earthy browns on its back."

"It lay so still."

"I asked you to touch it but you were scared. Do you remember? You wrapped both arms around my legs and squealed."

"I remember you placed it in the underbrush and *then* I wanted to touch it."

Mac turned to Seth, "She's really an outdoor person."
"Still is."
I stood up. "Do you mind if I go and see Kate?
Mac's chin tilted up. "I think she'd like that."

It was cold out here. I leaned on the railing next to Kate.
She spoke first. Empty. "You're not drinking?"
"I promised." I glanced sideways. "You asked him?"
"This morning."
"Why here?"
"We were talking. It happened."
"I thought you would be pleased it's over."
She grimaced. "How?"

"What did he say?"
"I'm not sure he believes me."
"He does."
"How do you know?"
"He's been waiting for you to ask for a long time."

She was angry. Hushed, bitter words. "He's doing this—he's trying to hurt me."

"No, I don't think he is."

"So why is he acting like this is just another family vacation?"

"Because he cherishes the memories of this place and because he wants a divorce. He's relieved."

"Relieved? Is that how he feels about our life?"

"You should ask him."

A heavy wave crashed below. Was Kate's request one of spite? It's a foolish motive. *You should know.*

She sighed. "In there, what Mac said about you and hiking," she looked defeated, "that's the man I loved."

She wanted the divorce. Mac was fine with it. Kate didn't know how to respond.

I was suddenly tired. "Don't you find this a little absurd?"

"It's not what I thought it would be."

"You weren't trying to hurt Mac by asking for a divorce?"

She shook her head. "No…"

"There's a lot of chaos in my life. But this, what Mac said in there, and what you just told me about how he reacted, how you are reacting, it's a little like Alice in Wonderland."

She tried to smile.

"What if divorce isn't the end?"

She flinched.

"What if this is a good thing? What if you two are happier with each other outside marriage?"

"I don't understand."

"I'm not sure what I'm saying. I'm pretty screwed up. I can't live up to Seth's expectations."

We stared into the darkness.

"I've hurt people. You won't understand. I'm not sure I can stop myself from doing it again."

"What are you saying, Andie?"

"I can't stop. You know…"

"How bad is it?"

"Bad."

"You need help."

I shivered.

"Do you want to go inside?"

I shook my head. "All I see is inanity. Coming here, I expected more."

"We didn't disappoint."

I put my arm around her shoulders.

"I'm sorry I put you and Seth through this. We shouldn't have wasted your time."

"Thank goodness for Alice."

"She's been your favourite for a long time."

"Since I was ten."

She sipped. "Don't you think we all live down a rabbit hole?"

"The question is how each of us chooses to live inside our madness."

As Kate twirled her glass I placed my hand next to it. *Christ, I need a drink.*

She sighed. "I can't find a way forward."

"Do you have to? Right now, I mean."

"I thought I was ready for this."

She sipped again.

Grab the fucking glass from her, drain it and stick your tongue inside and lick all the drops out.

I tried to lighten her load. "I prefer to remain distant and unengaged."

She stared.

"Let me ask you something."

Kate closed her eyes.

"Do you think Mac has changed, over the years, I mean?"

"Some. It's too late."

"He's trying even now, isn't he?"

"Maybe. Doesn't matter. I did more than my share. I sacrificed fourteen years at home with you while Mac built his businesses. His old school beliefs would have held me hostage longer if I hadn't decided to go back to school."

"You left him many times."

"Over and over, but I couldn't do it. I packed our bags more than a few times. I made arrangements for us to move to Brandon."

"Brandon?" The image of *Shelter-lady* mushroomed. I felt a rush of panic. "You never told me."

"I wanted to. But each time I realized it would hurt you."

"Maybe it wasn't Mac who held you back."

"It was."

"Kate…"

Kate shook her head. "Don't."

"You resented him for his chauvinistic ways but I was the one pulling your apron strings. How could you not resent me?"

"Let's not talk about it."

"I'm not blaming you."

"I wasn't a bad mother."

"Of course not."

I felt her withdraw.

She whispered. "We should go inside."

"I'm sorry. I shouldn't—"

"No, my girl. Thank you."

"For what?"
"You're not as cynical as you'd like to think you are."
"Give me time."

HIKING

I woke up angry. At myself. At Kate and Mac. I scrunched the duvet around my neck and closed my eyes. Seth puttered around in the kitchen. Last night was a waste of time. It's your fault, Seth. You want things to be nice and clean and neat. I tried. Shit. Life isn't like that. Did you see what happened? That's what pretending is like. Do you want that? And why was I so *fucking* nice to everyone?

It wasn't long before the aroma of coffee drifted into the bedroom.

Better to stay in bed than confront my drinking habit. That's what it is, a habit? I made it through yesterday. You can't stop me from drinking, Seth. I might make it through today. But you can't stop me. Last night, that glass in Kate's hand, I was manic—I'll do anything for a drink.

The hike today will help. I want to show Seth the ridge. I want to show him the trail where I used to go to feel good about myself.

He arrived with coffee and his morning smile knowing better than to talk to me. Two cups of java are a minimum before I utter anything human. I sat up, adjusted my pillows and rested the warm cup on my tummy.

"I'm going out on the deck to people watch."

I grunted.

As he walked away and slurped I noticed the faraway look in his eyes. Melancholy. There's nothing I could do. Didn't feel so good myself. *Don't want to go home. Remember when you liked to be alone?*

Seth was still on the deck when I climbed out of bed. The ocean was white-capped and angry and the morning light, muted by clouds that hung heavy over the bay, made we want to bury myself under the bed covers.

"Hey."

He looked cold as he turned around.

"You need your sweater."

I threw one at him and plunked myself down.

"You awake yet?"

I stared half asleep out into the Pacific.

Below, a small dog, maybe a beagle mix, sprinted along the path to the beach. He crossed over a ridge of sand and logs just as a man in his twenties emerged below us calling out, "Pupper! Pupper!"

Several beachgoers pointed in the direction of the dog. The man ran in pursuit. By now the dog, still running hard, had worked its way a few hundred yards along the shoreline. Sand kicked up behind him as his legs fought the shifting ground beneath. The man shouted and whistled. The dog veered shoreward and stopped. His ears spiked.

Another shout. A tail wagged. The dog took off, sneaking looks back whenever he heard his master's voice. The man stopped. He whistled. The dog spun around.

The young man began walking slowly back towards the resort, never looking over his shoulder.

The dog's bark was ignored. Yelps could be heard across the bay. A tail wagged and the dog began to trot back, slowly at first, resisting the pull of his master. He trotted a few steps farther. He stopped and barked, his appeals ignored.

From up here we could see the man smile to himself. He whistled and the dog moved from a trot to a full gallop and when he finally reached his master the dog raced past the man before arcing in a tight circle and jumped into waiting arms.

I emptied my cup.

"Interesting."

"Can I have another?" I held out my cup.

Seth pulled himself out of the chair. We watched as the dog continued to lick the man's face.

From the kitchen. "They played a game, both knowing how it would end."

He handed me a hot cup of coffee. "Question is, who is master and who is servant?"

I sighed.

"You okay?"

"I'm a mess."

"We need to go on that hike."

I looked up. "Can we stay?"

"As long as you want."

I wrapped both hands around the cup and stared out as a boat of whale watchers slid past the bay moving into open waters.

"How's the melancholy?"

"It's the weather—a trough of low pressure's coming in. It's almost fall."

"Your favourite time of year."

"There are times during fall that I fill up with so many emotions I think I might burst."

"Including the sadness that comes with shorter days?"

"Especially the sadness."

"It changes you."

"In a good way, mostly. Sadness makes me reflect on things."

"Like?"

"Melancholy has a way of separating the important from the frivolous."

"But you are enjoying yourself here?" I asked.

"I wasn't looking forward to—who wants to watch a train wreck?"

"Everyone."

"No." He shook his head. "I expected ambivalence from Kate. I thought Mac would crush me with testosterone fueled stories of mergers and acquisitions." He glanced my way. "She asked for the divorce?"

"Yeah."

"You okay with it?"

"Let them go their own ways."

"Don't tell me you don't care."

"Even if I did?"

He tilted his head.

"Yes?"

"I didn't know you liked to hike? I want us to do this more often."

"I don't think so, Seth."

"You can if you want."

I headed inside. "Let's get something to eat."

Early in the afternoon a westerly pushed clouds away. Cox Bay glistened to the delight of sea-goers relishing a late summer afternoon. We packed our bags and stored them in the truck. Seth picked up lunch from the kitchen and we headed to the beach. A biting wind forced us to walk backwards at times until we reached the shelter of the ridge. For a while we walked alone inside ourselves. Under these overhanging firs a feeling of safety, of freedom, that same feeling when I was fourteen, it was inside me again.

A makeshift path wound its way from the shoreline to the ridge above. "This way." Strewn with stumps and logs tossed helter-skelter this route made for hard work.

"You know where you are going?"

I ducked under a long branch. Seth was already puffing.

"We'll climb to the ridge and then walk until it curls and faces out to sea. We can have lunch there."

Loose boulders stuck out in the dry soil that coated our boots in brick coloured silt. Branches torn away by winter storms littered the ground. We climbed slowly. I stopped and looked back to the resort. Seth absorbed in his thoughts, seemed ready to say something.

I waited.

"We're an odd couple."

"Who says we're a couple?" I shook my head. "You know you're entirely obvious."

He fumbled. "I mean… in the sense we drift along beside each other with no plans always assuming the other will be there."

"Works for me."

"Hanging out must mean something?"

I started off. Seth hopped over a log. An older couple breezed by, power walking as if inside a mall, oblivious to this tranquility and the happy chirps of children below.

"I think hanging out means we're good," I said.

"Like today?"

"Like today."

"That's all good if it's only the two of us."

I stepped over a large boulder.

"I've been thinking of Rom."

"I miss him too, Seth."

"Can you imagine him here? He'd find a spot all his own." He stopped and peered between branches obscuring the beach.

"And these winds…"

"He'd be in his glory. You wouldn't be able to tear him away. Andie, I promise, next time it will be the three of us." His soft eyes gained some urgency. "He can give you purpose."

"That's what I'm afraid of."

He picked up a long, bending stick gnarled at one end in the shape of a fist. He stuck the gnarled end in his palm and looked at me. "Was that Andie being honest with herself?"

I started off again.

Seth walked with his back and head arched toward the sky.

"What are you doing?"

"I feel like an explorer."

"Come on. A few minutes more."

He huffed. "If we're going to hang out I want Rom to be a part of what we do."

"I'd like that." I wanted more of Rom than I dared admit.

Below us waves crashed onto the rocky shore.

He continued. "It seems to me that you pretend and you pretend. Why are you so afraid?"

"Afraid? I'm afraid I might go mad."

"I don't understand." He waited for me to respond.

I didn't.

He continued to launch the walking stick in front, testing the earth before our steps.

He changed the subject. "Rom often goes swimming on Sunday afternoons."

"He can swim?"

"No. He stands chest deep watching the other children splashing around him. He holds his hands above the water so the splashing doesn't hit him in the face."

"The water is too cold here for him."

Seth laughed. "Too cold for anyone."

Large fir branches swung lazily overhead and higher in the trees the wind sliced through thinning branches.

Seth was lost in thought.

I stopped. Back there, the resort was nothing more than a dot inside a lush rain forest.

I pointed. "Remember when we hiked there the first night?"

"Yeah."

"And I pointed across the bay. This is the place where I said we should build a house."

"Actually, it was me who suggested we build a house."

"Whatever."

Seth propped the stick under his chin. "I don't believe you're cynical."

"I'm trying terribly hard."

"Despite your attempts I see someone who, dare I say… believes."

"Oh, Christ. Shut up."

"Are you going to drink again?"

"Jesus, Seth—"

"You've been thinking about it."

"Of course."

"You can't continue—"

"Don't start…"

"I'm worried."

"About what?"

"About us. About Rom."

"You take care of Rom. I'll take care of myself."

"And you and me?"

"I'm not making any promises."

"Rom might be sad, or scared or happy but he's in the moment." Seth grinned that silly grin of his. "He helps me. I don't have time to focus on the machinations of trying to impress others."

"Neither do I."

"It's why you two get along."

We started off again.

"Maybe."

"You never impose yourself on him."

I laughed. "I save that for you."

"He loves you, Andie."

He continued. "He makes me think about things."

"Like?"

"Happiness doesn't come from wanting other things."

"Are you ever sad he can't be like other children?"

He shook his head.

"Doesn't it hurt you to see him so fragile?"

"We're all fragile." He poked the ground with the stick. "I want the best for him. But don't you see—even if I wallow in pity for my son, I do it without him. He doesn't feel sorry for what he doesn't have. He might be teased at school and feel rejection, but he moves past those feelings better than you and me.

"Oh, I know."

"And when he relishes the beauty in this world, the simple things, it's magical."

"Like out there." Here the ridge opened up and the trees gave way to an expanding vista. The power and majesty of the Pacific roared at our feet.

Neither of us said a word. A few hundred yards out a fog bank drifted towards the shoreline.

"I don't want to go home, Seth."

LET ME TELL YOU A STORY

It was after four before we started home. Seth slept. I drove an empty, winding road disappearing from the coast. Above us treacherous, jagged mountains hovered as we twisted and swerved around thick slabs threatening to break away and crush us. There are no towns out here, no gas stations, no tourist traps, just the road and a few worn wooden bridges traversing an emerald river traveling alongside for miles. Eventually, the mountains gave way to gentle slopes of second and third growth forests in teals and hemlock. Here was the first hint my weekend was over, the grasping ambitions of humans fully evident in denuded hills, raped and abandoned by murderous thieves in the night.

Seth stirred. He tried to open his eyes.

"Have a good sleep?"

"Where are we?"

"Sproat Lake."

"What happened to the sun?"

"It clouded over after we left the resort. Rained a bit." Thick, heavy leaded clouds layered above the water.

He stretched.

"Want to drive?"

He shook his head and glanced at his phone. "Any reception?"

"Doubt it."

He put his phone down and adjusted his seat.

A small chop crested atop the lake. Above us gusts raced into the valley ahead.

He pointed. "Slow down."

"What?"

"Pull over."

"Why?"

I rounded a long corner and pulled up beside a concrete barrier on the edge of a gravel embankment that ran straight down into the dark, cold lake. Beyond, across the choppy waters resilient hills of ancient forests rose to meet the clouds in an unbroken unity of nature.

He whispered, "Look at that. It's an image that will imprint on you forever."

"I'm going to need it."

Even with the windows closed it was hard to ignore the winds, gusts growing angrier as whitecaps charged towards us.

"You told Kate she should have left their marriage when you were a kid."

"I did."

"Why?"

Light rain began to fall.

"I told her because she almost killed herself."

"When?"

The storm rumbled overhead.

"You really don't want to know."

And then a deluge battered by indignant winds shook the truck. It was impossible to see outside. Soon it was impossible to talk without shouting above the storm. Seth, pale and anxious, slid away from the window. The storm, over us now, came in waves, one after another, shaking the car. I closed my eyes and imagined we were inside a long, thin metal tunnel, vibrating as winds and rains assaulted. Our flimsy shelter rattled and shook. How long before parts ripped away, how long before we were exposed to reality?

Seth is right. I pretend and I pretend. It helps me shield myself from the shit of the world. I can't sit here and wait out the storms. In the everyday madness pretending I'm an instructor, pretending Seth and I hang out, pretending Kate and Mac don't matter, it helps me get by.

As fast as it arrived the storm pushed on. Slits of blue sky winked. A truck passing by honked. I honked and pulled out and we were off.

"Let me tell you a story." I said.

Seth clicked his seatbelt into place.

"When a child experiences trauma that is neither explained nor soothed by the parent, that child continues to live that trauma without ever being able to put it aside. You can't make the terrors stop. You *relive* it over and over, trapped in one horrific moment."

"It's what PTSD victims go through."

"Exactly."

Ahead cars and trucks slowed. A tree had crashed over part of the road. Traffic from both directions alternated past the fir. We rocked cautiously over mangled branches and fist sized rocks, edging along for a quarter mile before regaining speed.

"You needed help," Seth offered.

"That's your answer?"

"I don't know. I'm trying—"

"I'm self-destructing, Seth."

"I'm know. You can't—"

"When I was ten my parents fought every week. One night, I heard them arguing. Kate screamed at Mac. She kept screaming and screaming."

"About?"

"A few years later she told me Mac had been screwing around with his secretary. Kate caught them in their bed."

"Shit."

"The arguing went on and on. From the stairs through the opening to the kitchen I saw Mac laugh as he smashed a glass of whiskey on the counter. Kate punched him. He grabbed her around the head and threw her down. Her head cracked against a chair. A deep purple bruise welled over her right eye. Mac walked out."

"Did they see you?"

"No. I went back to my room. A while later I heard Kate in the bathroom down the hall. I heard things."

"Things?"

"She was crying. I heard what I thought were pennies falling on the floor. From the hallway and the light filtering under the door I saw her hand on the floor. It looked like she picked something up. I pushed the door open."

"And?"

"She was sitting on the floor, her left arm wrapped around the toilet bowl. Her face was a mess. The welt had swollen her eye shut. She didn't even look up at me."

"What was she doing?"

"Pills."

"What?"

"They were pills, not pennies, all over the floor. She stared, not knowing me."

"What did you do?"

"I started to pick up the pills but she grabbed my hand and squeezed it so hard I dropped most of them. The desperation in her eyes scared the hell out of me. Her fingers grabbed a few more pills. I kicked her hand and they fell out. I scooped up others, the ones I could reach before Kate shoved me. I ran into the master bathroom and flushed them down the toilet."

"Did you go back?"

"I stayed with her all night. I made sure she didn't kill herself."

"Oh, God."

"I fell asleep standing up. Did you know you can do that? I remember jerking awake. Kate, sitting on the toilet, glared at me through the mirror. Her glare seared so hot I welded to the floor."

"You were a child."

"Her words were bitter. 'You're the reason I want to kill myself. I'm still in this marriage because of you. You're the reason I want to kill myself.'"

Seth tried to say something but his mouth was dry. He tried again. "I'm so sorry."

"For what?"

"You didn't have to tell me."

"I did but I left something out."

He shook his head. "Don't."

"It's a little thing called time."

"What?"

A car slowed as it passed by. A trucker waved. Another tree, this time smaller, blocked the road ahead. I stopped. A couple guys got out of their vehicles and pulled the tree off the road. They cleared other debris while vehicles in both directions waited. Eventually, traffic from the other direction crawled past us and we were on our way.

"Time?"

"Over the years the wound closed until it was just a scar. The scar, still there, is a part of me like many other things. Healing. It's the healing. And time. Anyways, the important thing is I can think of that night now without reliving it."

We were quiet for a long time. Through the trees, blue sky and a setting sun dried the road. We were moving quickly now. Seth leaned against the head rest, staring without blinking.

The road was twisting and traffic slowed. I smirked. The storm over the lake, the winds battering the car, how suddenly we were alone.

I giggled.

He looked over.

I turned away.

"What?"

"We were afraid of the storm."

More giggles escaped.

Seth's smile turned a switch.

I couldn't help myself. Uncontrolled giggles erupted.

He guffawed. "Andie, don't."

I put a hand up, warning him to look away. My ribs began to throb.

A chortle burst from him. And another.

I doubled up.

He snorted.

I burst.

He burst. He roared.

I giggled.

A horn section run amuck.

I glanced over. Seth grabbed his ribs as snorts alternated in staccatoed repetitions, rising and falling, until spent he fell against the window.

We dared not look at each other.

An uneasy calm descended.

I stared ahead.

Beside me deep breaths alternated with ahhhhums. He was on the verge of losing it.

Tears rolled down my cheeks.

A snigger escaped. I couldn't stop it. I clamped my cheeks tight. My body shook.

Seth rumbled.

We were off again but this time all pretense of self-control was abandoned. We veered this way and that—Seth squealing like an angry seal. Unable to keep his breath he howled and gasped before oxygen deprivation pulled him back.

I honked like a French horn until my ribs ached.

It felt so incredibly good.

Slowly the symphony quieted until only our breaths could be heard.

We avoided each other.

I shook my head.

"What?"

"I can't—" A grotesque snigger escaped.

"Don't."

I gasped and held it. Finally, I could speak. "When we lost it the second time the most ridiculous thought occurred to me."

"What?"

"That I enjoyed this weekend."

"I know you did."

"And the most absurd thing happened."

"What?"

"I was a child again."

JAYMIE'S NEWS

I avoided Seth for days. Ignored his texts. What were we supposed to do? Tofino was an aberration. When I finally returned his call, he told me Rom was coming to stay for the weekend. He asked if I might stay over. I said yes, but it wasn't about Seth, I told him that. I had to see Rom.

Jaymie texted. Asked if I'd like to go for a drink after work. Why not? I had honored my promise to Seth. Besides, he didn't have to know if I had a drink or two. Jaymie and I were to meet at the Bengal Room. Said it was her treat, she had something important to tell me.

I was ushered to a window overlooking the rich lawns and immaculately trimmed roses. Jaymie was on her way. I ordered a merlot and studied the menu. Rumours were rampant the Bengal Room was about to close. The curry was tempting but when I sipped I knew I didn't need anything else.

My glass somehow emptied by the time she arrived. I ordered another. I told her about Tofino, about hiking and the freedom that comes from being away from all this shit. She seemed happy for me but there was something else, she was distracted. I wasn't sure what to say so I told her about Mac and Kate breaking up.

A wry smile formed around the corner of her mouth. "I have something to tell you."

She took a deep breath and when she looked at me, her eyes were haunted. "My life is just a little too tidy."

I played along. "I thought you liked it that way."

Bitter words. "John prefers order. I tolerate it."

"Tolerate?"

"I've tried. I can't—I won't do it anymore. He's on auto-pilot."

I looked away. *No kidding.*

She saw through me. "You've seen it."

"Of course."

"I need to be more than productive, more than a planner, more than a business woman."

"You are. Always have been. Jesus, Jaymie. It's so good to hear you say this."

"I want John to be passionate, to disagree with me because he sees more than who we are now, to get excited about new things, to take risks, to get out of the rut he's in."

"And he doesn't see it that way?"

"You know he doesn't."

"You have a comfortable life."

"I'm alone, *in that house.* The kids, they're beginning to think like their father."

"And they don't know how you feel?"

"That's the funny thing. John goes about his day, and I do my thing at the store, we share chores, help the kids with homework and maybe later we watch TV together. Nobody, not John, not the kids, know how disillusioned I've become. I'm lost. I'm totally fucking lost."

"It doesn't have to stay like this."

"It can't. I'm dying."

"What are you going to do?"

"First, talk to you."

I laughed. "Me?"

"You've known about this for a while."

I shrugged.

"It's only me, you know. John's comfy the way things are. He's never going to change. He's oblivious to my feelings."

"And the kids?"

"Bennett and Dan... they don't know any better. How could they? I've rarely given them a glimpse inside the me that I cherish most. I feel bad about that. I want to take risks and be scared. I ache for the freedom to imagine. I want the kids to think, no, I *want* them to feel like I used to."

"What kind of things?"

"Things John would choke on. I want to write poetry. I want to spend time *thinking* about running for public office. And I want to do real things, like volunteering at a shelter for battered women."

"Battered women? That's my... What's stopping you?"

"Me. It's me, Andie. I have no one else to blame."

"You can't do those things with John?"

Her head shook. "No. Never. I'm trapped. I'm forty years old. My life's over."

"Welcome to the club."

"Ah... we need to talk about you and Seth."

"Not tonight."

"The other night John was at the store. I was in the backyard raking leaves. The kids came out to see what I was doing. It was cold. Bennett couldn't wait to go back inside. I told her not until she lay down on the grass. She stood with her hands on her hips, like her dad does, she asked me why she would ever do that."

I laughed.

"I told them to lie down beside me. Dan did."

"And Bennett?"

"Eventually. You know what twelve year olds are like. She was worried one of the neighbours might see her."

Jaymie glanced at her phone and back at me. "I wanted to show them who I am. Silly I know, I'm desperate. They think I'm this aging, bitching mother of do this and that and be home by nine and don't think for yourself because it might be dangerous."

"That's not you."

"I asked them to close their eyes and take three deep breaths, then open their eyes and tell me the first thing they saw."

A waiter came by. I ordered another.

Jaymie declined.

Dan said he saw oak branches waving. It's only September but the wind was cold like it is after Thanksgiving."

"Did Bennett say anything?"

"She begged to go inside."

"Did you encourage her?"

"I decided she was comfortable in her teenage funk so I let her be. I asked Dan if he saw anything else."

I sipped.

"He said all he could see was a bunch of stars."

I chuckled. "At that point Bennett got up and went into the house."

"How did you know?"

"I teach young adults only a few years older than her."

"Dan asked me what he was supposed to see. I said it was up to him. The trees and stars and anything he saw were things he could explore. He could imagine the past or the future, the starts might be animals or art forms and if he wanted he might think of them as metaphors."

"How old is he?"

"Fifteen. He said he was hungry so we went back inside."

"Did he say anything else?"

"He went to the fridge and made a roast beef sandwich."

"No surprise there."

"Later, I was in my office when he knocked on the door. He was going to bed, kissed me and then on his way out he stopped. He asked me—"

"Asked?"

"He asked if we could hang out more often." She paused. "That's why this is so hard. They need me, Andie. If I walk out now they're going to think I'm abandoning them."

"And you can't do this and live at home?"

"John has no room in his heart for this. I understood the challenges when we first started dating. I tried. One night after work I took him skipping."

"What?"

"As a kid I loved to skip. So, I bought skipping ropes and enticed him to come outside. I thought he would see this part of me and things would be ok."

"And?"

"He told me to stop being so silly. He said he wasn't going to skip and make a fool of himself."

I sneered. "He's seen too much of that asshole Brent if you ask me."

"Nothing has ever interested him other than his business."

"Until you came along."

"And only me if I surrender to his ways."

"You can't do this anymore, stay and try and make it work?"

"I'm going mad. And if John had been home the other night he would have intervened and we would have fought. I'm not going to do this behind his back. I'm not going to pretend to be someone else. I'm not going to fight with him about what I know is right for me and the kids."

There was that word again.

She sipped and put her glass down. "I'm not sure John would notice if I walked out tonight."

My glass half was empty, the buzz reminded me why I drank. I flicked my hand to a waiter.

"Listen, Jaymie, I'm not exactly a model of great relationships. I don't have kids. I don't mind listening and I will do whatever you ask me but you're in a shitty situation."

"Let me ask you a question."

I put my glass to my lips.

"What makes you happy?"

I chortled. "You're kidding?"

"No, I mean it."

"You know, for a moment I thought you were Seth."

"He's good for you."

"Perhaps."

A waiter approached.

"Want something to eat?" she asked.

"Go ahead. I'm fine."

"You sure?"

I drank.

Jaymie ordered and she persisted. "What makes you happy?"

"Really?"

"Yes."

"Listening to you."

"Come on."

I paused. "Authenticity. The outdoors. Challenging the status quo. Peace and quiet."

"Anything else?"

"Seth and I hiked in Tofino."

"When was the last time you did that?"

"I can't remember."

She smiled a sad smile.

"It is what it is. But we're talking about you tonight."

"If I'm going to do this I need my best friend grounded and there for me."

"Ha." I put my glass down. "What are you going to do?"

"Talk to John and the kids on the weekend." Her voice shook. "I'm moving out."

"Where?"

"I found a one room suite in Oaklands."

"And the kids?

"I want them with me. Just not yet." She held the table with both hands, steadying herself.

"I know you can do this. The kids might not understand now, but they will. They're smart, they'll come around."

"I'm no good for them like this. Right now, they're not going to understand."

"How could they?"

"I'm being selfish. I have to, for them, for me."

She continued. "Anyways, John can't take care of them. Not by himself. He won't."

"That's what I'm saying. Bennett and Dan are going to end up with you."

That's what I'm most afraid of." She looked away. "I can't lose them Andie. I can't."

"Jesus. You know what you're doing. And the kids love you. Hold on to yourself. If you do, they will follow you."

I emptied my glass as Jaymie's dinner arrived.

MIXED COMPANY

I told Jaymie over and over she was making the right decision. She had to feel good about herself, she needed to find her old self, for her and for Dan and Bennett. We talked about making sure the kids understood they had not done anything wrong. Of course, that's impossible. When Mac walked out the first time, after Kate left my room, my only thought was what did I do wrong? And Kate, so caught up in herself, lost in her fears, was unable to soothe mine. I didn't dare ask her what I could do to fix things. I kept my thoughts to myself. Jaymie was determined not to let that happen with Bennett and Dan.

We agreed she should invite them over to her new place as soon as possible. I suggested they make a routine of weekly meals at her place.

I finished another glass.

Jaymie opened-up. She told me John had lost interest in sex about a year ago. He told her it was because of the store and the need to keep the business afloat. Besides, he said, things were different now with growing kids in the house, and it didn't seem right that he and Jaymie should get randy and fuck in every room like they did when it was just the two of them. She worried it was something else. In the last year, John had hired a young woman as part time help in the store. She was attractive and attentive to every one of his requests. Jaymie didn't like her and she was sure the feeling was mutual.

I asked her if she missed the sex. She said she missed being naughty, sex was a release from the daily grind. I didn't tell her I used sex as a back-up to getting drunk.

I was hammered enough that I believed I was doing Jaymie a favour by encouraging her to get it all out. She was exhausted and barely finished her meal. Later, she pushed the plate across the table. I nibbled.

As she ordered martinis I was reminded that marriage is the shits and I'm never going to indulge. At least Jaymie had the courage to get out.

I glanced her way.

She looked at me.

I couldn't focus. I smiled foolishly. "What?" I slurred.

"We've been friends for sixteen years."

My head was spinning.

She was in fine form. "I've helped you navigate out of bad relationships, two, no three? Was it Tony, the prick accountant, who wanted you to quit your job and move to Calgary so he could take a promotion?"

I laughed too loud. "The shortest relationship in my life. I was in a funk—"

"Over the previous guy. What was his name?"

"Tom."

"That's right. The double-barreled Tony and Tom."

Someone's voice cut in, "Jaymie. Andie! What are you two doing here?"

I looked up. A man in a suit, his tie tight around the collar, grinned confidently down at us. I tried to focus. I couldn't place him.

"Brent," Jaymie blurted. "Brent, what are you doing here?"

I guffawed.

"How was dinner?" he asked.

"I didn't eat."

"Hungry?"

I shook my head.

He turned to Jaymie. "Mind if I join you?"

"Sure." She looked nervously at me.

Oh, shit. He's barged right in like a brooding monsoon.

Brent leaned back in the chair and loosened his tie. "Do you mind?" He took his jacket off. "Long day. Too many meetings." A maudlin smile rolled past. I ducked under the nauseating wave.

He and Jaymie struck up an awkward conversation, strained words about John and Brent's fishing trip in the fall, and a false promise about having him over next time he was in town.

Brent ordered a double scotch. "Another glass of wine, Andie?"

"Merlot. Please."

He nodded to me. "I owe you an apology."

"Shit."

"Yes. I owe you an apology for the last time we met."

"I don't remember. Who are you?"

A soft smile came out of nowhere. "I made a fool of myself."

"The last time we met you couldn't stop talking about yourself."

"Yes, I did. I'm sorry."

He was trying to be nice.

"Who the hell are you?"

A soft smile again. "I knew you were smart. I found out you were more. I wanted to impress."

"You were an ass. You and… you boasted about the power of your lobby… you tried to put me down."

"I live in a world that does those things."

"That might impress others—."

"I apologize."

"Ok."

"Can we start again?"

I shrugged.

"Good then. First off, we won't talk politics."

"Ok."

"Secondly, I'd like to know more about you."

Jaymie sniggered.

He looked at her.

"Andie doesn't talk about herself. And right now, she's a little hammered so she's about to clam up."

"Ok, then. Maybe I shouldn't have ordered you another drink."

The waiter arrived. Brent ordered dinner.

Drinks arrived. I held mine to my numbing lips.

Jaymie was anxious. She glanced at her smart phone and texted. Conversations erupted then faded. We sat silent.

I closed my eyes. Losing myself.

I looked up. Above the entrance a tiger sprawled, eyeing everyone in the room. Tonight, this absurdity with Brent, the tiger saw it all. I had to get out. I tried to stand.

"Woah. Where are *you* going?"

A hand on my shoulder.

"I have to go—"

"Let me finish dinner. I'll take you home."

"Where's Jaymie?"

"Left a while ago. She had to pick John up from the store."

"Oh."

"You don't remember?"

I stared at the tiger. *Why aren't you helping me tiger? Can you stop him from being so nice?*

"Jaymie left and my dinner arrived. You told me about Tofino. It sounds like you enjoyed yourselves."

I stared straight ahead.

"You and what's his name?"

My words stretched out. "His nammmme is Sethhhhh."

"I told you about hiking above the hot springs in Banff and at Johnson Lake where anglers come from all over the world to fish for speckled trout."

"Do they catch anything?"

There it was again, that warm smile.

Brent chatted.

Later, he helped me up. We walked into the cold. It was raining, his coat around my shoulders.

"Jaymie says you're the best of friends. I'd suggest she's lucky to have you in her life."

"Where are we going?"

"To my car."

He ushered me into the passenger seat, my face smooshed against the window. Spinning. Shit, no way he's taking me home. The streets sped by, rain sliding down the windows, a night disintegrating.

"We're almost there."

"What?"

The car stopped. He pulled me out, bundled me against him.

"Where are your keys?"

"Purse."

He fumbled. Keys jangled.

He laid me down on the couch. My heels slipped off.

"I shouldn't have drunk so much."

"Why is that?"

"I promised."

"What kind of a promise?"

"I promised him I wouldn't drink."

"Do you have any music?"

"Ohhh, Stones!" I tried to sit up. "Play *Miss You*."

He went across the room.

My eyes closed. I laughed. "I don't like you."

Mick ranted. Music thumping, bumping, humping…

"I like you."

I felt him above me.

Tried to open my eyes. Couldn't. "You just want to fuck. I know how to fuck, you know. But you can't fuck me tonight."

A warm hand caressed my forehead, pushing hair from my face.

"You can't have me unless I want to fuck and I don't want to fuck."

"I'll leave now if you want."

I shook my head.

"You shouldn't get drunk, Andie."

"I like to… Hey, Wild Horses. *I know I dreamed you a sin and a lie…*"

Warm lips pressed against mine.

A soft sensual kiss.

"Move over."

I shifted against the back of the couch. He came down beside me.

"Hold me." I buried my face into his chest. He smelt good.

"Can I stay?"

"No."

He kissed me again. My hand rested on his thigh.

You're sinking into repugnance. You do this when you drink. I know, I know. I hate myself. I fucking hate myself.

I opened my mouth, our tongues met. He put his arm around my back and pulled me tight. His passion turned to my cheeks, my neck and to the opening of my blouse.

You're bereft.

The hunger in his eyes flashed and then—the ego of that night at dinner. The bully.

"Shit! Get off me." I twisted away from him. "I just realized something."

"What? I thought you liked—"

"No… I'm drunk." I stood up, tucking in my blouse.

He lay there, his eyes begging. "We don't have to stop. You're so beautiful."

"You're such an ass."

"Don't say that. I'm not. You know I'm trying to be nice."

"Nice, my ass. You think banging pussy is the same as exerting control in your corporate world. But you forgot one thing Brent, I'm in control. Do you understand?" I straightened my hair. "You're a Neanderthal. A fuckin' Neanderthal."

"You don't want me to stay?" He whimpered like a teenager.

I started down the hallway to the bathroom and stopped. "Thanks. That was a good try. Too bad for you. There won't be another."

ALL CONTRADICTION

I missed work Friday. Too hung over. Slept most of the day. Kept thinking about Mac and John and Brent, pricks like Tom and Tony made life hell for women. Except, none of them intended so. They just did. They imposed themselves on my life because that's what men do. There's still no equality of the sexes. Not even close. A man's a man and nothing has changed.

The problem as I see it, a problem that has existed before the time of the religions, is that women have purposely born the pains of the inequalities, have known that they could do better, and over time, at least in the last seventy years we have done better, but we've not done enough. Have we? And why is that? Why haven't we turned away the tides of male dominance and sexual predation, why haven't we squelched financial inequalities in the workplace?

It's not because we are the ones who bear children. And we're not weaker. It's not because we can't. We can but not until we find a new way. And not until we stop pretending we are men. Look at Kate. She could have done things differently. Instead, she joined the men's club and left her marriage and before that left her daughter so she could advance her career. Well, shit. That's exactly what men have done for centuries. So, until women find a better way to equality, I'll continue to live inside my distant and withdrawn world.

I wondered if someone from senior faculty would come knocking about my absences. Didn't care. Losing my shit, drinking again, knowing I would hide all of this from Seth—why the hell did I care about a job?

When I got up in the noon hour I only wanted one thing. My nerves vibrated. I couldn't fight the urge. A couple of glasses, that's all I needed. I drank most of the bottle.

Seth texted to remind me about dinner. I laughed. Christ. He said he was picking up groceries and would drop by Melissa's to endure a lecture before bringing Rom home.

I went to his place and let myself in. I tidied up, washed and dried the kitchen counters, filled and started the dishwasher. The kitchen table lay chock-a-block with books. Seth's laptop lay open. His manuscript, a never-ending write and re-write, would never be finished. He didn't have it in him. It reminded me I had yet to do a lick of research on a paper required by faculty. Might start in the new year. The first draft wasn't due until April.

I heard a key in the door. Rom pushed it open with both hands, stood in the light peering into darkness.

"Andie! Andie…" He ran to me and wrapped both arms around my waist, giving me a hug that wouldn't let go.

I melted.

"Ok, Rom. Andie wants you to let go now."

Rom looked to the floor where various toys were scattered. "Andie, come play."

"How about you get a book?"

He shook his head. "No. Play with me." He unzipped his backpack and pulled out two miniature racecars.

"What's that, Rom?"

He held them higher for me to see. "Cars."

"Are those yours?"

He nodded proudly before handing me a green sportster with white pinstripes.

"Very nice," I said.

Rom held the red car to his cheek.

"Is the red one your favourite?"

He nodded as he dropped to his knees and began to drive the car round and round the carpet, circling faster with every lap.

"Andie, play with me."

I couldn't bring myself to be with him.

He talked excitedly. "This is my racecar. I'm the driver and I decide how fast and how loud the car can go." He leaned hard on the car pushing it into the carpet to the point the wheels stopped spinning.

"Rom, don't push so hard. Be gentle, let the wheels turn."

He turned in Seth's direction. "The wheels are broken, Daddy."

"No, son. You're pushing too hard. Hold the car gently and let the wheels turn."

Rom pushed the car over the carpet and across the floor as the wheels spun faster and faster. "See Daddy, I did it!"

"Yes, you did."

He grew bored and climbed up between Seth and me on the couch resting his head against his father.

"Are you tired?" I asked.

"No, Andie. I want to sit with you. I'm glad you came to dinner tonight."

"Are you hungry?"

"I haven't eaten since lunchtime. I had a very good lunch today. Mom made me a cheese sandwich and I ate all of it because I was so hungry."

I reached out and held his warm, soft hand. His fingers wrapped around mine. His soft breaths perfect.

He glanced at me. "Are you going to help with dinner? Daddy likes when I help him."

"Yes, I am. You can play and we'll call you when dinner is ready."

Seth eased his arm from around the boy's back.

"Can I listen to my book?"

"It's in your backpack."

Seth turned to me in the kitchen. "You cleaned up."

"Yeah."

"How are you?" he asked.

"Fine."

"You look tired."

"Thank you."

"What's wrong?"

What could I to say?

"How was your night with Jaymie?"

"She's good."

"What did you talk about?"

"Not much."

"I'm asking."

"We had a girl's night. Caught up on the last few weeks."

"Did you tell her about Tofino?"

"What about Tofino?"

"Did you tell her we had a great time?"

"Sure we did. Mac and Kate coming apart."

"You know what I mean."

He put his arm around my shoulders.

I couldn't look at him.

"Have you been drinking?"

"No."

"You're cranky."

"I'm back at work."

"You haven't been drinking?"

My voice rose. "Jesus, I told you."

"I thought you wanted to see Rom."

"I do."

"You sure?" He pulled veggies out of the fridge and handed them to me.

"I'm tired, Seth."

"Ok, then. Let's start over."

"I'm sorry."

"Rom's been looking forward to dinner and this night with you. He talked about you non-stop in the car."

"I thought about what you said in Tofino—about seeing more of him."

"And?"

"We should hang out more often."

Seth's face was a mix of disappointment and elation. "What do you mean?"

"What I said. Let's hang out more with Rom."

He turned away to work on the chicken. His chin dropped to his chest. "Rom will be pleased."

I knew he was hurt.

He changed the topic, told me that business at the restaurant was slowing, two of the servers were to be let go at the end of the month. He loves his work, the crazy pace of a busy night, finessing the final touches to a dish, Seth excels in this environment. He hates the cold realities of lay-offs. His boss wants to keep Seth on because he has talent. He doesn't want to lose Seth to the competition. I suggested that wasn't necessarily a ringing endorsement if business remain brisk. He agreed. He knew he was next to go.

As I finished prepping the vegetables he jerked his head towards Rom. "Play with him."

I dried my hands.

"I don't have any wine tonight."

"That's fine."

"Glad to hear you say that."

I ignored him. Except, I couldn't. I was about to sit on the floor with Rom when I stormed back into the kitchen.

"You can't stop me from drinking."

"What?"

"You can't stop me."

"Don't raise your voice."

I turned away.

"Andie." His voice was soft. "You don't have to do this."

"You can't stop me."

"I know."

"Then why didn't you buy wine?"

"I'm sorry."

"You can't control me."

"Listen to yourself. You came here to be with Rom."

I heard my voice threatening, "You don't dare—"

"Look at him." He gestured a hand towards the boy. "He sits and plays with his cars but he's waiting for you."

"You don't know that."

"He's been waiting all day. You're all he's talked about."

I felt Seth's hands on my shoulders. "Go to him."

Rom held one of the cars upside down in his hand, spinning the wheels over and over.

Seth soothed, "He knows you're unsettled."

I wanted to hit back. I bit my tongue.

Seth came over and sat down in front of Rom who immediately handed him the car.

"Play, Daddy."

"Ok. Show me your car. What's it doing?"

On his knees Rom raced the car in circles across the carpet, around Seth and under the coffee table, in an expanding loop, the wheels barely touching the surface of the carpet as he gurgled the sound of a racing engine.

He bumped into Seth and looked up. "Daddy's turn."

Seth mimicked his son, racing the car over the carpet. Every movement Seth made widened the boy's eyes in single-minded devotion. This mattered. Seth changed course and turned the car in my direction, racing it up my shins to my thighs and travelling my arms to my head.

Rom roared, a loud, uninhibited laugh. "Daddy's racing, Andie. Do it again."

Seth did. And again, and each time Rom celebrated, my body tingled.

Rom looked to me. "Andie is happy?"

"Yes, Rom." He came to me and we hugged. I held on.

He took my hand and led me to the floor. We played with the cars and listened to the radio. He took me to his room and I read to him. After dinner, I tucked him in and he wrapped his hands around my neck and kissed my cheek.

Later, lying next to Seth, I tried to find that feeling but it was gone.

I wondered if it is too simplistic to think I might someday gain control over the incalculable forces inside me; contradictions of fear and apathy, hope and despair, mashing up in a ball so entwined that not only is it impossible to unravel, it is impossible to know what I might feel next.

I am, in any instant, coming apart and seeking happiness but unable to understand how, if ever, I might hold on. I don't know how to embrace life—even as Rom embraces me with his perfect love.

I want to be like Rom. He might not know why he is like he is but that's the same for most others. I'm determined to never to let myself enjoy me. Lying, blaming others, shirking my responsibilities, cheating myself of the joys of honest relationships—oh, I'm very good at those things, as addicted to those behaviours as I am to alcohol.

I'm not afraid of the consequences. I don't care about consequences.

Something else, a single thought in the dark caused me to break into a cold sweat—I'm addicted to losing control.

In high school, Beth and I thought we were bold and dangerous when we snuck into libraries late at night. The exhilaration, our hearts pumping against our ribs, the thrill of almost getting caught made us want to do this drug again and again.

An easy high. Jesus, if she could see me now.

SENIOR FACULTY

When I walked into my office I was surprised to see Associate Dean Murray waiting. Then I remembered as I glanced at my smart phone. Ten minutes late.

"My apologies. Got lassoed by a student on the way in."

Richard nodded politely.

"How much time do you have?" I asked.

He was business-like. "I have about ten minutes."

I put my things down and moved over to my desk.

Richard straightened himself. He peered at the papers in his lap then glanced back to me. "You know your probationary period is coming to an end in the new year."

Staring blankly at him I forced Richard to look down at his papers.

He mumbled. "This meeting is customary when an employee enters the last few months of probation."

"Did I need to prepare for today?"

"No. I'm here to inform you of the views of senior faculty regarding your work. I also have a written report summarizing our findings."

I stared without emotion.

"Ummhmm."

He looked down at the report, trying to be less formal but he couldn't. He sat rigid. His words stumbled out.

"Our committee feels your work over the past eight months has been adequate. You have met the minimum criteria in your teaching assignments. Your frequent absences are a concern." He glanced at me and back to his notes. "The committee feels your continued absences may jeopardize your consideration for future work within this faculty. In addition, your research is lacking. Finally, your contributions to the university and the community at large have not lived up to your contractual obligations."

I asked coldly. "What does that mean?"

He hesitated. "It means… it indicates that you must address your lack of research and engage yourself in university/community activities, both in the next six months."

He tried to be supportive. "Where are you with your research?"

"Not far. I'm stumped by an approach."

"Have you met with your advisor?"

"You mean, Mary?"

"Yes."

"Well, she's about to go on maternity and she's been busy teaching, as I have. We talked about getting together before the end of the year."

"That would be a good don't you think?"

Oh, shit. I'm being reprimanded.

"Yes, I suppose."

"Have you given any further thought as to how you might get involved directly in the university or broader community?"

"I'm sorry Richard, I haven't."

He shuffled the papers, his eyes flittered to the window. "I see."

I offered a token. "I'll set something up with Mary."

"Good idea."

He raised his hand to his mouth and coughed politely.

I pulled him to me until our eyes met. "Is there anything else?"

"Andie, I don't want to be harsh but there's a feeling amongst staff that you are disengaged in your teaching role."

"I see. Is that your opinion as well?"

His looked away. I locked on until his pale green eyes shifted back.

"Let me say this," his voice barely a whisper. "The university may end your probationary appointment at any time."

Shit, was this old-school top-down scolding supposed to mean something?

I waited.

"Umhmm. You understand what I just said."

"Perfectly."

"There are concerns—I'm sorry to have to be so blunt."

"No, not at all. You have your job to do. I appreciate you coming to my office to meet with me."

He reached into his lap and placed the report on the desk. I ignored it and stood up, came around and extended my hand. "My apologies for being late."

He stood up and walked out as quickly as his short, little legs could manage.

I closed the door and put my hand to my mouth.

Holy shit. What the hell was that about?

I opened the tiny cabinet next to my desk. A bottle of Merlot waited. I plunked it on the desk and picked up the report. As I sipped I flipped through a few pages before sliding it over the edge into the trash bin.

I drained a glass of wine and picked up my phone. My fingers tapped.

Seth. Just had a laugher with senior faculty. I was supposed to be intimidated by an arrogant white-assed, old man who still believes in the rules of academia. Can you meet for a drink? I know, I know, one glass, that's all. I want to tell you all about the interrogation.

Ttyl.

Oh, where are you at with your draft of your book? I can help with research if you like.

SETH AND ME

Our taxi grumbled up the hill, along Fort Street past Cook, squeezing through narrowing lanes that make room for bikes that seldom come this way, past stately Victorian houses occupied by non-profits for partisan reasons, leveling out at Fernwood before proceeding along a newly-paved road, finally tight around a treed corner and up one more incline before flattening out at the lights at Pandora. It was dark and the light was red.

Seth's head rested back, eyes closed. In an indeterminate moment, I saw stubble on his cheeks red then tinged with green, as this city, this tiny universe, peered inside the cab and time stopped.

I slid beside him. His eyes opened. Surprised, he sat up. I kissed his cheek. His arm went around me and we were tight.

We kissed, lips warm, aching.

I pulled away.

"What was that?" he asked.

"I'm sorry. I shouldn't have—"

"We can."

"But I'll hurt you."

"Don't say that."

I moved to the door.

"And we can't talk about it?"

"Do you want to?"

He winced. "You do this awfully well."

"I lie a lot."

"You lie to yourself a lot."

"Yes, you've said that before. In Tofino, you said I pretend and I pretend."

"In Tofino you said you don't like yourself very much."

"It's true."

His hand reached for me. "It doesn't matter how I feel?"

"Not unless you want to be hurt."

"I think we passed that signpost long ago."

I stared out on the street.

"I think I'm a pretty smart guy, Andie, but it's hard for me to know what's real."

"Maybe we shouldn't see each other anymore?"

"Is that what you want?"

"I'd die."

"Why say it?"

His weary eyes begged me to come to him.

"Because Tofino was a dream."

"But we were together."

"You're a romantic, Seth." I reached out. He covered my hand in warmth.

His words soothed. "We've been together longer than we have been with anyone else."

"You never give up, do you?"

He grinned his goofy smile.

The cab pulled up to the pub and we got out.

"I can't believe I agreed to drink with you."

"We're just having a few."

"You can't drink, you can't—"

"We're just hanging out."

"You and me. That's all I want, Andie."

"And Rom."

"And Rom."

I told him about the visit from senior faculty. He told me not to dismiss the visit outright.

"Why?"

"Because they might suspend you. What if they don't renew your contract?"

"Can you imagine how little I care…?"

Still upset about what happened in the car earlier, he didn't hear me. He changed the subject.

"Mac said something to me when we were in Tofino."

"When?"

"You were on the deck with Kate."

"What did he say?"

"That our generation has nothing to live for. He was bitter, like he resented us."

"The only things Mac resents are people with more money and bigger houses."

"I suppose that's a measure of a life."

"Did he say anything else?"

"He said we have everything we want and nothing to achieve. He said we're too easily satisfied and we don't know how to overcome adversity."

"What did you say?"

"I told him every generation has something important to fight for."

"Let me know when you find out what it is."

"You don't think he's right, do you?"

"Of course not."

"I'm thirty-four, you're forty-one and compared to most our age, life has been easy. So maybe he's right."

"Mac doesn't know what he's talking about."

"I'm saying that we come and go whenever and mostly wherever we want. We have fewer burdens than our parents."

"Fewer?"

"We care less for material possessions, we don't covet status, and jobs don't define us."

"We may be like that but most who live in our part of the world are not. It's just Mac, he generalizes like most old, white men who see the world from a diminishing perspective."

Seth persisted. "Our generation does have a different set of values."

"If Mac was less preoccupied with himself, he'd worry more about the generation behind you and me."

"Why do you say that?"

"Am I the only one who sees a whole generation of YouTube oglers sitting on their fat asses passively dreaming that they might get lucky?"

"Lucky?"

"That they might become famous if famous means acquiring status online. Shit. Is this where the next generation of leaders is going to come from?"

He sipped his beer, put it down and asked, "Who said they want to be leaders?"

"Our generation has taken a pass on leadership. We've decided we don't need to make the important changes this world requires. Those behind us have seen the future and they don't like it much either so they sit in front of their glass screens and hope by doing nothing they can become famous."

"You read books."

"You're not comparing Tolstoy and Dickens to two minutes of self-indulgent acts of *'Hey, look at me, I'm different'*—You can't be saying that Seth McCallister."

"I'm saying you lost yourself in books when you were young and dreamt of a life different than the lives we live today. Isn't that what the YouTube oglers are doing?"

"Books educate. Books liberate. Books challenge the status quo."

"And YouTube videos don't?"

"You know how absurd you sound?" I put my glass down. "The more a kid sits in front of her computer the more likely she's missing out on a world that requires hands on to make real change."

He laughed.

"What?"

"This is Andie speaking? Am I hearing you or is there somewhere else inside?"

I finished off my glass.

"You'd make a good mother."

"Doubt it."

"I have something to tell you." His face lit up. He paused.

"What?"

"Rom's coming to stay with me for a few months."

"You're kidding?"

"Melissa and I agreed yesterday. Two months to start."

"When?"

"Not sure. Soon, I hope."

"And she's ok with Rom staying with you?"

"It's her idea."

"What happens when you're working?"

"We have a care-giver."

"You're ready for this?"

"More than ready. Rom is too."

"I guess I'll be seeing more of him?"

Storm Rolling Into Darkness

"Actually, I have an idea." His eyebrows danced.

"What?"

His head tilted playfully.

"You're kidding? No way. You want us to live together?"

"Why not?"

"What the hell are you thinking?"

"You can be with Rom."

"I know, but—"

"He loves you. Come on, Andie."

"No way. No way are you and I living together. It's a bad idea."

"Bad idea?"

"It won't work."

He was hurt, again.

"I want you to think about it."

"I have."

"I mean it, Andie. I don't need your answer tonight. Just take some time and think about it."

I ordered another. Inebriation settled in. The rhythm of booze flowed through my veins. Animated thoughts flowed.

"We should go camping," I said.

"You want to go camping?"

"I don't know. I just think we should go camping more often."

"Andie, we've never been camping."

"I'm going to bring Rom to class with me. He can watch me teach. He'll be mesmerized by the sounds of voices inside a lecture hall."

The more I talked the more I liked my ideas.

My words sprinted. "I'm not moving in with you. I know it's what you want but it's impossible. You don't know me. Why did you think I would agree with that? I have a better idea. Rom's coming stay with me. You can't. We'll be friends and we'll plot behind your back."

"Plot what?"

"I don't know. We'll create plans to sneak into libraries at night."

He laughed. "You've already been a thief in the night. And Rom should join you?"

"Of course. He needs to absorb the thrill of adventure. But you can't come. It's going to be our secret."

Later in a cab I thought of Seth and Rom. Seth's devotion lights Rom up. And with the two of them together, I'll see Rom more often. But I'm not moving in. I don't understand how Seth thought I would agree to such a ridiculous suggestion. It's impossible for me.

The cab pulled up to the curb in front of my condo.

"You can't come up tonight."

"No?"

"No."

He tried to go back to earlier tonight. "What happened… in the cab on the way to the pub—"

"I'm sorry."

"I'm not. I'm not at all because I know something."

"It won't happen again."

He didn't try to hide his enthusiasm. "We'll see. I don't think you can stop what happened tonight."

"I didn't mean to hurt you."

"You didn't. For a moment, we were together."

"Almost."

"I can't come up?"

"It will confuse things."

He kissed my cheek. I moved to the door. We kissed again, this time a peck on the lips. I stepped out. Those big blue eyes were still hopeful. I put a hand on the door to stop me from going back to him.

The cabbie asked Seth where he wanted to go. He didn't answer. He looked at me as if he remembered something.

"I dreamt about you last night."

"What kind of dream?"

"We were hiking. It was an early morning and we walked on a field of grass thick with frost and our heels kicked up crystals twisting lazily in the morning sun. Our breaths pushed out in front like fog against the horizon of a new day."

"Where we were going?"

"Together. We were going together."

"That's nice." I leaned in.

"We didn't speak. We didn't have to. You looked content."

"I wish."

"I felt it inside you."

I shrugged.

"Tonight wasn't a dream, Andie."

"I have to go."

In the condo at the window I looked out. I felt him too. The cab was running, the door still open. Wiper blades flicked in the night. A hand reached out and the door shut and the cabbie pulled away and drizzle fell across the back-window fragmenting Seth into slivers of darkness and light until no human form could be seen.

In that moment, forever in my mind, we perished together.

I poured a drink and turned out the lights.

CLASS

Sipping water from lips numbed by booze, head bowed, arms and hands like jelly, I sucked back until the world swirled and I blacked out. When I came around I didn't know what day it was. And then the alarm on my phone went off and my head shot up. Class in a half hour. Shit. Alain's away this week.

Stumbling across the commons, and inside the building, I pushed the door open to the classroom. To my left a rumble of feet and mindless banter reminded me these privileged shits were here to notch another lesson in their belts.

They ignored me. In the front row a young man glanced at his phone. I stared. He started to type, both thumbs poking clumsily, his head shaking at the typos. I stood over him. He didn't look up until I tapped the chair.

"Shall we begin?"

I placed a sheet of paper on the lectern and pretended to scribble a few notes while I waited for the chatter to wane. It didn't—except for my admirer—it was Mitch, wasn't it, who followed my every move. I put my hand up.

Words tumbled out of my mouth. The din faded. They waited. Too juiced to think straight I couldn't remember the topic.

What are you doing, Andie?

"Does anyone have any questions?"

There were none.

"No questions? Ok, then."

Murmurs fluttered. I looked down at the paper. I stared, not sure how long. Unease swallowed the room.

"Excuse me," someone shouted.

I tried to find her voice, a young woman standing in the middle rows. "Are you ok?"

"She's stoned," someone shouted.

Titters of laughter.

"Very funny." My cheeks burned. I couldn't make the spinning stop.

Feet shuffled.

Someone walked out. Others followed.

I wrote *fuck you* on the paper. I couldn't look up, pushed hair from my face, too embarrassed to run, too humiliated to rescue any dignity. The room emptied.

Except for Mitch. His soft blue eyes were just like Seth's.

Seth, last night after you dropped me off I drank until I passed out. It's the only way to forget about what I would do to us if we lived together.

Mitch moved towards me, his lean, youthful body looked like something I wanted to taste.

I smiled impishly.

He hesitated.

I heard myself, "I need to go home. Want to take me?"

His eyes shifted nervously. "Yes, if that's ok with you."

"I can't drive."

"We'll take my car."

I barely knew the kid, gave him my address, dropped into the seat and slumped. The intoxicating smell of new leather distracted from my pie-eyed hell hole. We didn't say much as the car speed through the streets. Mitch was shy. I was too drunk for small talk. He liked to drive fast.

"Can I park here?"

"Huh?"

"Can I park here?"

"Where are we?"

"Your place."

I pushed the car door open, tried to stand but fell back into plush warmth. Mitch helped me up, his arm gently around my waist. I fumbled in my purse handing him my keys.

"Which one?"

"The shiny one."

He opened the front door, held it for a couple walking out, then ushered me inside. He put the key back in my purse.

"No, don't. We need it for my door."

"You've had too much to drink."

"Just a little."

He slipped the key inside the lock and turned it as the stench of stale wine pushed past us. I pulled him in. The door slammed hard.

I looked up. "Thanks."

His mouth curled. Hesitation flooded.

I kissed him hard wrapping my arms around his chest. He didn't respond. A lingering kiss. His arms around me. My hands roamed down his back to his ass. He pulled me tight. Long lingering kisses. Christ, I wanted him. His hands came away from my hips. I waited for him to feel me through my skirt. Instead, he pushed me, away.

I laughed stupidly.

"We can't… I can't do this, Andie."

He said my name. I tried pulling him to me. He was too strong.
"You brought me home. I have to thank you."
"I can't."
I jeered, "What is it—afraid your girlfriend will find out?"
"I have to go."
I kissed him hard and he weakened. Another kiss more intoxicating than the last. I reached for his hips. He spun away. "No! Don't."
What's wrong with you? You don't like me?"
"I do."
"Don't you find me attractive?"
Yes, yes. I didn't think we—"
"Mitch doesn't like to fuck?"
"Don't say that."
"What don't you want, Mitch?"
"I brought you home. I wanted to make sure you were safe."
"Safe? Jesus. I'm begging you to fuck and you want me to be safe? Is that it?
"I'm sorry."
"You're sorry? Get out!"
He slipped away, footsteps scurrying down the carpeted hallway. I slammed the door and locked it.

When I turned around *Shelter-lady* stood in front of me, her red, messy hair and sad blue eyes reminded me of Kate's humiliation when the others stole her dignity. Now I was Kate, a laughing stock, a drunken fool who needed to hurt herself again by throwing herself at a kid half her age.

Shelter-lady walked away.

RUNNING

I stayed drunk. Passed out. When I came to, I drank. Mitch made me a fool. He knew what he was doing. Didn't matter, I'd soon be out of the job I hated. Good for me, too bad Mitch. You miscalculated. I don't feel bad about coming on to you. You wanted it too. Why else would you drive me home? You're a conniving little shit. Good luck with life. Let me know if you find anything significant.

Where's my goddamn phone? It's not in my purse. Is it in Mitch's car? Did you steal it, Mitch? If you did, I'll press charges. Where's my fucking phone?

A glass of red rested in my hand. As red as the bruise on *Shelter-lady's* cheek. How many other bruises were hidden under her clothes? How many times did she cower from a man whose threats kept her on the run? She kept running and I had to keep drinking. Kate told me *Shelter-lady* dragged her kids from city to remote town to another province and back again, seldom staying in a location for more than a few months, most often grasping at part-time work or seasonal positions. She remained wary, always on the look-out for *that* man until finally her ex was in custody for beating another woman.

While Kate was open about *Shelter-lady*, she never talked about herself. Her withdrawal became mine. Even when Mac came home and life went on as if nothing had changed, Kate was never the same. We talked at the dinner table about our days, about the mundane, never about our fears. Mac left us again and then Kate walked out, and each time we came together we pretended. It just got easier.

And then I realized—how could we be happy when we had never been?

Mac obsessed about plans for summer vacations, preparing months in advance, relishing in the details that would unravel on the afternoon we arrived at the resort. Eventually, I understood this was his way of evading the day-to-day realities of a flawed marriage.

They entertained often, nights where booze flowed and loud voices recoiled in mock horror at adulterous stories. For a pre-teen these fermenting ingredients stirred a pot to boil. I was drawn to alcohol. It transformed the adults, I wanted it to do the same to me. It was the stories that sunk deep, especially from the men, huddled, laughing and puffing cigars, ignoring me, while bragging about their latest infidelities.

One night, a fat bastard I'd never seen before, glanced nervously at me, sipped his beer and was about to say something when Kate shoed me away. I was bored anyways so I wandered upstairs. Outside my room I heard voices, a woman laughing, a man conspiring, his deep voice uttering crude words. I watched from the shadows as they lay naked on my bed. He was on top, grinding his body and she moaned and wrapped her legs around him, and he moaned like her until short of breath he collapsed.

I fell asleep in my parent's bedroom. Sometime later, I awoke in the dark when Mac came into the room with Kate. He held her hand and whispered. She tittered and shussed him. I saw their shadows. It wasn't Kate. She kissed him. He was unbuttoning her blouse when I stretched and yawned. Mac jerked her out of the room.

I wandered down the hallway and poked my head into my room. It was empty now. Closing the door I crawled into bed. Down at my knees I found a pair of panties, tossed them on the floor, turned on my side away from the noise downstairs and fell asleep.

Where the hell is my phone?
Kate called. Or did she? What did she want? I can't phone back. Shit. Mitch, where is my phone? I'll hunt you down. You can't fuck me anymore, Mitch. Not now. I want my phone back.

I stumbled to the cabinet. Two empty bottles stared back. Grabbing my purse, I rushed out, running down the street like *Shelter-lady* not knowing where I was going.

A taxi drove by. My arms waved.

Brakes lights pumped.

"Take me downtown."

Across the bridge into town young couples sauntered arm in arm after a night out. They look foolish. Do they have any idea what the hell they are doing? Stupid, stupid fools. I'm not jealous. I'm not. But falling in love when you are young is like believing the first draft of Seth's novel is a finished product. It's never finished and relationships between men and women are simply drafts in need of a lot more work. It's not worth the effort.

I spotted a smart phone retailer and told the cabbie to stop. Inside the store I forced my way past a babbling, happy family. A line-up queued. Standing too close behind the man in front of me, he turned and glared. I glared. He turned away.

An array of phone products hung conveniently on a glass wall but I stared incredulous at the woman staring back at me. What happened? Your hair? Your ashen face, those bloodshot eyes—you're so fucking angry. I turned away.

The clerk, an insolent, uncaring prick, stared down over top of his glasses. His high, annoying voice dripped apathy. "How might I help you?"

"I've lost my phone. I need you to find it."

"What's your number?"

"My number?"

Sarcasm. "Yes."

I couldn't remember. I told him my name. "Look it up."

He glanced briefly at the others in line.

"Are you serving me or them? Find my fuckin' phone."

He tapped into the computer. "I have four people with the same name. I need your number."

I remembered, wrote it on a piece of paper and threw it at him.

"Is your location service on?"

"How would I know?"

"If it's on we can find your phone. If it isn't, we probably can't."

Head down he searched. "I can't find it."

"Try again."

"I did."

"Where's my fucking phone?"

"Excuse me?" A male voice roared from behind me.

My hand reached for the computer screen.

The clerk grabbed my shoulder. "You can't do that."

"Watch me." My hand twisted the screen. He pushed me. I slipped and fell to the floor.

His voice squeaked, "I told you, I can't find your phone."

"Hey, bitch." A large man in blue jeans and jacket hovered over me. "You heard the man. He can't find your phone. It's time for you to leave. Or do you want me to throw you out?"

He turned to the others and laughed bravado.

I pulled myself up. A forearm nudged me towards the door.

I wandered past Birks Jewelry along Broughton to Broad. At the window of Paggli's I peered through subdued lighting into the cramped restaurant where waiters served some of the best Italian food in the city. Dazed, my mind blank, I stared. And then I saw them—Jaymie and Seth sharing dinner. She gestured with her hands like she does when she's happy.

I collapsed to the sidewalk.

Seth smiled at her. His face gentle.

I screamed. I screamed and I screamed. My guts spilled out. I pounded the window. Everyone inside turned. To me. Jaymie's head shook in disbelief. Seth rose from his chair.

He came out and I struck him on the chest.

"You fucking bastard… Liar!"

He put his hands up to protect himself. I tore his shirt, ripping the buttons. A trail of red scratches ran down his pale, flabby skin. He grabbed and held me and I screamed so loud I couldn't hear his words. I bit his arm and he let go and I ran.

I ran and I ran and all the blood poured out of my heart onto these dark, cold, unfeeling streets.

When I stopped on Wharf I leaned against an iron railing overlooking a parking lot sixty feet below. I leaned over. It would be so easy—"

"Andie!" Seth waved frantically. He ran, zigzagging between vehicles splashing red and white. I raced down the block and across the street into Bastion Square, slipping down an ancient alley onto Government and through another alley on to Johnson.

A cab rolled by. I climbed in.

"Where to?"

"Just drive."

I glanced back. The street was empty of traffic and humans. I snorted triumphant.

COLD

On my back, on the deck in the rain, the nightmares were better than waking up. Cold, I crawled inside. Shivering. Yanking a blanket from the couch, sleeping on the floor, if sleeping means throwing up, my left arm corralled the vomit until it soaked up my sleeve and the stench woke me.

I hurled but nothing came up.

How long had I been drinking? The radio said it was Saturday. When was the last time I slept in bed? When was the last time I wasn't drunk?

I had to stay pissed.

Last night in the taxi I told the cabbie to take me to my office. An icy rain fell. An anxious feeling scratched inside my limps. What if I've lost control? This decaying body, a rotting mass, less human more animal, no longer alive still breathing, an unbearable *Weltschmerz*.

I didn't hear the cabbie when he pulled up outside my office. He shook me. I unclenched my fingers from around my purse and forced myself out.

Everything forced.

The long gleaming hallways and the offices were abandoned by the nameless leaving me alone with the person I despised most.

What if this isn't me? What if inside my office I can forget? But the door was open and everything inside could be seen out here.

Everything exposed.

Inside I crumpled to the floor, my cheek against the hard, icy tiles. I stared along a row until the wall broke in. Rain ticked against the window. Blinking. Separated from all that came before. *You feckless shit, you can't stop what comes next. There's no way out.*

Pulled myself up to the desk. Ah, fuck. My cell phone lay under an envelope addressed to me. I cupped the cold metal and glass. And stared. Disconnected.

The phone buzzed, incandescence forced me to squint. A text from Jaymie. There were others, Seth too. I read them. Running away? Kate left two voice mails asking me to call. I dialed her number. She didn't pick up.

I snatched the envelope and I ripped it open.

Attention: Andie Elaine Burrows

We wish to inform you that due to frequent violations of faculty policy, including teaching under the influence, you have been suspended until further investigations can…

Fuck 'em. I've wanted out for a long time. This is my chance. I don't need this. I don't need you, Seth.

Tried seducing Mitch. Cheated with Brent. Sex is my back-up. It's easier. It just hurts more afterwards. Coming on to Mitch… I'm ashamed. Far more ashamed than last year when I fucked a man I didn't know who was so kind in his throaty bravado to offer to bring along a friend next time. Lying in bed I watched him hike up his jeans, pull his t-shirt over his head and walk out the door without a word.

I laughed. I had to because when the door clicked and I was alone, I realized I was going to die like this.

You know what, Seth? All I've ever learned from love is to be the first one out. Do that and it doesn't hurt so much. At times, I thought we were a couple. How can we? When I'm like this? I got canned. What would I tell you if we were a couple? But I don't have to tell you, do I?

WE ONLY HUNG OUT, RIGHT?

I rang Seth's doorbell. Impatiently three more times before he cracked the door open.

"Andie?"

"Can I come in?"

He shook his head. "You can't come here when you've been drinking. Where have you been?"

I lied. "I haven't had anything for a couple days." I peered around him into the living room.

He inched the door tighter and whispered. "You can't see him. You've been drinking."

"I've had a rough time."

"Where have you been?"

"I'm not sure."

"Jaymie and I have been trying to contact you."

"Can I come in?"

Seth peaked over his shoulder.

Had Rom heard my voice?

"Andie, please. You need to go." He studied me. "You look terrible."

"Why didn't you come for me?"

"I did. We did… Your place was a mess."

"I'm not sure where I've been."

"What happened?"

"I don't know."

"What do you mean?"

"Can I see Rom? I need to see him."

He shook his head.

"I've been on a bender. I don't know how long but I haven't had a drink in two days."

His eyes softened. He whispered. "I'm not trying to punish you."

"Ok, have it your way." I turned to the street.

Rom let out a whelp. "Andie. It's Andie, Daddy."

Seth squeezed bitter words through the gap in the doorway. "You're killing yourself."

"Bullshit. I'm fine, thank you very much."

He ripped the door open and hovered over me. "We can't do this anymore."

"Do what? Hang out?"

Rom cried out. "*Bullshit. I'm fine, thank you very much. Bullshit. Bullshit.*"

Seth raced into the house. Rom held his hands over his ears, his head shook back and forth. Seth pulled him in, holding the boy in his arms. Rom repeated my words. Again. And, again.

Seth, glared at me.

Rom was terrified.

I turned away as Seth scooped Rom up and carried him to his bedroom.

I waited a few minutes then went upstairs. At the end of the hallway I heard Seth's calming voice. "It's ok, Rom. It's ok."

"*Bullshit. Bullshit.*"

"It's over now. You're ok, son. You're ok."

"I'm sad, Daddy."

I stepped nearer to see Seth kiss his son on the cheek. "It's over. No more fighting. Ok?"

Rom was inside a storm he could not stop. Then he saw me. His hands went to his ears. His head shook.

Jesus. I stepped back.

"I know my boy. I know."

I left them alone. Seth soothed. Rom fell quiet. Later, I peered into the room as father and son entered a ritual where Seth whispered short stories about their day together. Rom giggled. He held his father's hand.

He spotted me and slipped a small hand from under the blanket. He waved.

I waved back.

Seth kissed Rom on the forehead and whispered good night. He turned out the light and angled by me without a word.

He was downstairs when his hushed voice demanded. "Andie…"

In the living room I sunk down on the couch.

"Don't ever come here drunk again."

"I know."

He couldn't hide his anger. He spun away from me, glancing upstairs. " Oh, Rom. My boy. I'm so sorry."

"Seth—"

What were you thinking?" He disappeared into the kitchen.

I lay down on the couch. At some point, I was asleep when I felt a blanket tucked around my body. I curled tight against the couch.

When I awoke the room was dark except for the light from Seth's computer slanting across his face.

"What are you working on?"

"My manuscript." He stood and stretched. "How are you feeling?"

I pushed shaking hands from under the blanket.

He dropped down beside me.

"I knew it was coming."

"Lucky you."

"I had nowhere to go."

He pushed hair from my face. "Stay, tonight."

Awake for hours my mind reeled. Even in exhaustion I was desperate. Get out. Go home, get drunk—kill the withdrawals.

Nightmares stabbed—Mitch stood over me asking why I never come to class anymore. I stood with my back against a long, white paneled fence as a German shepherd bared his teeth inching closer. I screamed. Later, Seth held Rom in his arms, rocking him over and over as the boy, inconsolable, cried out every time I came near.

Dawn came to another day. This one I feared more than any other. I paced and drank coffee. Nerves vibrated to a crescendo then halted mid-beat. A wave of exhaustion forced me down.

Mid-morning, Seth came downstairs to find Rom sitting cross-legged on the floor next to me while I cooked breakfast, a bacon and eggs fried ensemble.

"Good morning my boy. How are you today?"

"I'm happy, Daddy because Andie is making us breakfast. I'm so hungry. Are you hungry, Daddy?"

Seth kissed me on the cheek. "Any better?"

I couldn't look at him. I reached into the oven and dumped baking powder biscuits onto the counter. "I hope Rom likes biscuits with butter and jam."

"He will. You made them."

A rush of despair made me want to cry out.

"What?"

I shook my head.

I said little during breakfast. My mind hunted for snippets of the last few days. When was the last time I taught? A vague memory of me in my office flashed. I needed a drink. Rom kept watch over us, wary for signs of discord. My nerves jangled at Seth's calm.

I couldn't do this. I pushed a half-eaten plate away and went upstairs to shower.

Afterwards, I waited until the mist cleared from the mirror. In my youth, my skin was smooth and supple. Now a translucent sheen made me look old. My eyes were uninhabited. My hair was thinning and as I combed it small clumps fell out. I examined my breasts. They were flat and hung low against my ribs like doughy masses—old lady's tits now. My belly, thick with booze fat, rolled in waves of neglect. I examined my ass and laughed. It hung unimpressive and lumpy like my breasts. Even my legs, my short thin legs were skimpy pylons holding up a decaying building teetering over a rising tide.

As I came downstairs Rom was in his glory. Flat on his belly on the floor next to Seth he pushed his racing car round and round the coffee table. I felt his joy.

Am I so lost I can't go to him and hold him in my arms? I'm broken, Seth. I'm incapable of loving another.

Seth closed his computer, glanced at Rom and then at me. "Do you want to talk?"

I shook my head. "No, not now. How?"

"Rom, do you want to go to your room and read?" Seth asked.

"Yes, Daddy. Can Andie come with me?"

"Andie has to help me on my computer. She'll be up shortly."

"I'm going to listen to a new book, Andie."

"Which one?"

"It's your favourite, *Alice in Wonderland.*"

My heart sank. If only... "I'll be up as soon as I can. We can listen together."

When Rom was safe inside his bedroom I mumbled, "You want to do this? He'll be listening."

Seth was determined. "I lay awake most of the night thinking about us, about you and how I can help you change. It's no use, no matter what I do, you fight back. The harder I try, the more you push me away."

I clasped one hand inside the other to try and stop the shaking.

He continued. "I'll take the blame. I'm not good for you. I've enabled your drinking."

I grinned maliciously.

"You think this is funny."

"I think you and Jaymie have plans that don't include me."

"What the hell are you talking about?"

"Don't lie to me. You've always thought she was for you."

"Andie, I've only wanted..."

I hissed. "What were you doing with Jaymie at the restaurant?"

"John's being a prick. He's building resentment in Bennett and Dan towards their mother. They're angry she walked out. I was there to listen." He paused. "You know, she's been trying to get a hold of you."

I turned away.

"We're worried. You're worse."

"You can't help me."

"Why do you do this?" He came around the table. "You pretend we don't matter but you call and text and invite me over to spend the weekend. You hang out with Rom. We had a great time in Tofino. And then you show up on my doorstep drunk?" He couldn't hold the disappointment. "You can't see him anymore. We can't do this, you and me. I'm sorry."

Over Seth's shoulder Rom stood at the bottom of the stairs, gripping the bannister with both hands.

Seth turned. "Rom, come say goodbye. Andie is going away."

Rom ran into my arms. "Bye, bye, Andie."

He held on.

I couldn't let go.

"I like hugging Andie."

My eyes locked with Seth's.

Rom stepped back. I brushed his hair with my hand and kissed the top of his head.

"Then, this is it?" I asked.

Seth looked away.

My phone rang.

He couldn't look at me.

"We only hung out, right?"

I pulled the phone from my purse. It was Kate. Closing the door behind me I moved out onto the street.

KATE'S NEWS

"Kate? Is that you?"
"Andie, where have you been?"
"I'm not sure."
"I've been trying to reach you for days."
"Drugs, Kate. I've been on drugs."
"That's not funny."
"Maybe not to you."
"Why haven't you called back?"
"I did but you didn't pick up." I sat down on the curb.
"I have to talk to you."
"Jesus, Kate. Not now."
"Andie?"
"What?"
"You sound tired."
"Exhausted, Kate."
"I have bad news."
"What kind of bad news?"
"I might have cancer."
The smirk ran away from my face.
"What do you mean?"

"I was doing a breast self-exam and noticed something. It didn't feel right."

"A lump?"

"Something's there, I don't know. I called my GP. She told me to come in."

"When?"

"Last week. The mammogram didn't reveal any abnormalities so she's arranged for an ultrasound."

"And?"

"I just received the results. There are suspicious areas."

"What do you mean?"

"I need a biopsy. I'm sick, kiddo."

I went numb.

"Will you come with me?"

"For the biopsy?"

"Yes." I glanced back at the house. Seth stood at the window watching.

"Do you know what kind it is?"

"What?"

"What kind of breast cancer?"

"I don't know. No, no… I won't use those words."

"When do you go?"

"I'm waiting to find out. Next week, I hope."

I heard myself say, "Next week?"

"I'm scared, Andie."

I choked back my fears and changed the subject. "Where are you?"

"At home."

Seth was still at the window.

"You'll come then?"

"When?"

"Next week."

"Ok."

"Thank you, my girl."

My girl? Something in her words made me—ache for her. "Sorry I didn't call back earlier. I lost my phone." There was no response. "Kate?"

"Yea." She paused again. "I'm having overwhelming feelings right now."

"What kind of feelings?"

"The sound of your voice, I want to be with you."

"Me too."

"Andie..."

"Yes."

"I'm going to need you."

"I know."

"It's good to hear your voice."

"Kate..."

"Yes?"

"Call me if you want to talk."

"I will."

"Bye, Kate."

I pulled myself up and turned back to the house. Seth raised his hands as if to ask if everything was ok. I nodded, got in my truck and drove away.

A gentle rain fell turning traffic and roads into a homogenous blur. *Focus on what's in front of you. Don't look back. You'll lose yourself.*

At home, I undressed in front of the mirror and performed a breast exam. Twice. Then realized I didn't know which breast Kate identified as the culprit. I texted. It was late before she responded. Left breast. I was in bed. I re-examined my left breast and texted back, *'Did a breast exam, didn't feel any lumps.'*

She *lol'd.*

I lay awake with pillows propped up. Eyes closed, my hand came to my breast. How delicate. I held it and dozed off. Kate texted. She asked if I would think about coming to stay with her for a while.

Jesus.

We talked every night. I was usually in bed when her call came. She said she liked to sit at the kitchen table and talk, that's where both of us solved many of the dilemmas of my early teenage years. She reminded me about the night when I was fifteen and came home drunk. I tried heading straight to my bedroom but Kate took my hand and we sat at the table. A bottle tucked under my jacket fell out. I caught it before it hit the floor. She laughed. She didn't know the bottle came from the liquor cabinet.

She said I cried that night and she consoled me.

"Wasn't it about a boy?"

Her voice was weary. "At the start of grade ten you went through a different boy every week."

I protested but couldn't remember.

"You were obsessed with boys. Every Friday night you came home either jubilant or in tears."

"It doesn't sound like me."

"After Thanksgiving you regained your sense of self.

"You mean my distance from others."

Kate sighed.

"Tired?"

"No… yes, a little. I'm sorry, Andie."

"Sorry for what?"

"Mac and I were a mess in those years. I wasn't always there for you."

"To be honest, Kate, I was so inside myself I hardly noticed. Even at school I hated the bittersweet crush of school popularity. At home, I could be alone with me."

I heard the kettle coming to a boil.

"I don't want to do this Andie—the cancer, I mean."

"We're not there yet. The biopsy—"

"It's the waiting." The kettle came off the boil. "It's dreading the words that are going to come out of the doctor's mouth. I can't stop thinking about what she's going to say."

Dread. There was that word again. What if I can't stop—

Kate's voice interrupted. "All this shit ahead of me. I'm not sure I can."

I laughed. "You sound like me."

"I'm not alone, am I?"

"I'm here. "I stared at my skinny legs. *I'm not alone.* I let her ramble. I wanted to hear more about the past, my past. It held more promise than tomorrow.

"Andie?"

"Sorry, Kate."

"I was saying I should probably let you go. It's late."

"Try and get some rest."

"I doubt it."

"My phone is beside me if you want to talk."

"Thanks, my girl. Night."

I was falling. Had been for a long time. In the last few months I crashed through one safety net after another. I had lost any fidelity I had with Seth. How was I to know my descent would be stopped by, of all people, Kate? Wasn't she the one who tapped me on the shoulder one night and said everything was going to be ok—before our lives changed forever?

Distracted and absorbed inside Kate's fall I forgot about mine. I was the only one who understood her, her vulnerabilities. Maybe, it was simply, I was grateful she had broken my fall. Maybe, I understood taking care of Kate was something I could do.

I texted Jaymie. Told her the news about Kate. I ignored the night at the restaurant, didn't tell her about my drinking. No, I avoided all that by asking her how she was doing. Asking Jaymie about her situation was easier than talking about mine. She texted back immediately. Things were rocky with the kids. They still wouldn't come over to her place. Instead, she met them at the house while John was out. She cried after every visit but she was firm in her decision to leave. I told her that we needed to meet and catch up. She said she would make the arrangements.

I wrote Seth a note. A note with a stamp was better than our shared history of habitual texts. I told him about Kate's biopsy and I was moving back home to care for her. I could imagine the look on his face. It was the right thing to do. And Seth was right about our relationship. It was time to break it off. Us together, it's too hard on him. As difficult as it is right now I insisted Seth move on with his life. I asked him to give Rom a hug from me.

At the corner of the street I pushed the envelope into a mailbox and went home to pack my bags. I felt like shit. Of course, I did. I didn't tell Seth I'd found sobriety, however long it might last.

DIAGNOSIS

The house smelled exactly as it did when I was fourteen. The oily warmth of hardwoods mixed with the ferment of books languid on dusty shelves. I stood in the foyer thinking so little had changed, wondering what the hell I was doing here. The grandfather clock *tick-tocked* in the same location on the wall outside the dining room. Pictures on the walls in the same places, the furniture, wool carpets, everything looked like I had just come from school.

Even the liquor cabinet I stole from gleamed in an angular winter sun. I had mixed feelings. Already, too many bad memories mushroomed. This was going to be shitty. *You're here for Kate.* That's what I kept telling myself.

Cancer diagnosis is a marathon of emotions and will. We waited. The biopsy took place Monday morning. Dr. Borden called Kate to come in Thursday afternoon. I could never take the call without insisting on the results. Kate didn't ask. She said she didn't want to know.

Just after lunch on Thursday I went to get the car. I decided to be my disinterested self, thinking when we faced the doctor I would be in a better position to help Kate. But when I pulled into the driveway and saw her standing at the top of the stairs my heart sunk. She stared defeated, the creases on her face rigid, knees buckling as she disintegrated down the stairs.

The faint, sickly odor of lilac hung heavy in the cold waiting room. Kate stared at the floor. There was nothing to say. Anything would be forced and foolish. She took my hand and covered it with damp disquiet. We waited.

I watched her comb her hair this morning. She took her time using long, measured strokes creating a sheen that when combed back gave me the impression of a woman in her prime. I knew little about her childhood days in Brandon. I knew less about her high school years in North Van. She met Mac in first year at Cal Berkley. She told me about the psychedelic LSD scenes and the protests, about Mac playing *Surrealistic Pillow* over and over until she discovered *Sgt. Pepper's Lonely Hearts Club Band*.

The chaos of those hedonistic days seemed a lot more certain than this one. I wondered what it was like to be the doctor on the other side of the door who came to work every day to provide wretched news of disease to distraught humans. Teaching college students seemed wonderfully optimistic by comparison.

Kate broke the silence, her mouth pasty. "How's Seth?"

"Fine. He's working longer hours."

"And the little boy?"

"Rom."

"He has autism?"

"Yes."

"Poor child. How's he doing?"

"He's doing well. In many ways he's an inspiration."

"You should invite them over to the house."

"Let's do this first."

The door opened and Kate was called. She went rigid, a self-preservation rejecting the moment. I helped her into the office. The door clanged behind us.

Dr. Borden was a small woman. Immaculately dressed in sweater with a crisp collar, a pleated woolen skirt draped below her knees. Calm, personable, she ignored the file resting in her lap and spoke directly to Kate.

"Thanks to both of you for coming in. I know this isn't an easy time but I'm pleased we were able to get the biopsy done so quickly." She addressed me. "Andie, thank you for coming. It makes a big difference when Kate has the support of her family."

"I expect you have bad news for me," Kate said.

Dr. Borden's words seemed oddly reassuring. "I'm sorry, yes I do. Kate, you have invasive lobular carcinoma. It's the second most common type of breast cancer. As the name implies the cancer has spread to the surrounding breast tissues."

"It sounds bad."

"Not necessarily. There are some very successful treatments that have worked for many women in your situation."

"There are options?"

"Some yes, of course. None are going to be easy. We will need to work together, form a plan and get after it. You're going to have a lot of people in your life from now on. These are smart, dedicated women and men who know this isn't what you wanted but are there for you at each step you take."

Dr. Borden stopped. "Ok?" She waited and when Kate nodded the doctor continued.

"Your treatment will be tailored to your cancer."

"Tailored?" I inquired.

"In most cases, surgery is the first course of treatment. Based on the results of your biopsy," she looked directly at Kate, "I would recommend a mastectomy."

"A mastectomy?" Kate stiffened.

"I'm sorry, yes. The cancer is Stage IIIA which means the mastectomy will remove the breast and most likely some lymph nodes." She paused. "Kate, we need to be aggressive."

"A lumpectomy is no longer an option."

"Unfortunately, no. We're already beyond a lumpectomy and a partial mastectomy."

Kate glanced at me then asked. "What else?"

"Following the mastectomy tissue samples will be tested and then chemo therapy is likely your next step."

Kate squeezed my hand.

I heard myself say, "This is not what we wanted to hear Dr. B."

"I understand. I'm sorry." Dr. Borden remained calm. "I'm pretty sure we know what we're dealing with. But I understand that this is a lot to absorb."

Kate walked to the window clasping her hands together in front of her. "I know you don't have the answer but I have to ask." She looked across a courtyard to the road where cars waited at a red light. "I'm used to legal wranglings which can go on for months, sometimes years. I suspect this is what I'm about to face?"

"Yes, you will have months of treatment and rehabilitation. I don't mean to be trite but we'll take these first few steps and see how things go, see how far the cancer has retreated."

Kate turned and tried to smile. "Thank you."

"As I said, I know this is a lot to take in." Dr. Borden glanced at the report. "I want you to think about what we're discussing today. And call me if you," she looked at Kate and then me, "if either of you have any questions." She looked back at Kate. "Having breast cancer doesn't mean you can't work. It doesn't mean if you need to cancel travel plans. Cancer is only part of the amazing woman I know you to be. And, it's better when you are with someone like Andie. You're a formidable team."

"Do we have much time?" Kate asked.

"I don't think we do. This is the first step. We don't have all the answers quite yet."

The calmness in Dr. Borden's words betrayed reality. Kate has cancer. She might die. The tips of my fingers were numb.

Kate looked at Dr. Borden. "We will…" her hand squeezed mine, "talk tonight over dinner."

The doctor's lips pursed into a smile. "Good then. Enjoy your dinner. I'm ready to get to work when you are."

We waited for the surgery. Kate had more meetings. I researched nutrition and recovery options for breast cancer patients. We read aloud to each other on the impact of chemotherapy. We laughed at our obsession with getting her treatment and recovery right. How ambitious of us—until now we couldn't build a decent relationship.

I insisted we focus on the procedures, on the mundane, the pragmatic grind that would keep us steadfast on the horizon but the worry in Kate's eyes never went away. This was supposed to be about her return to her former life but the trouble is life is never linear. When we had a clear path to the surgery Kate came down with a cold. The surgery was postponed.

Three weeks later the surgery was within reach. Part of me didn't want it to happen. Taking that step opened the door to a whole set of unknowns. *What if it doesn't work, what if some other surgery is required, what if she needs more chemo, what if chemo doesn't work?*

Another nightmare ran over and over in my head. I never mentioned it to Kate. Strapped and blindfolded inside the sterile cart of the health care system she was about to be catapulted down a claustrophobic tunnel of unforeseen twists and turns, never stopping, never ending. And the irony? Treatment was the grease on the wheels. Her life was out of control, an unwilling passenger in her own decline.

Oddly, our lives became routine. Most days we were up early, a breakfast of juices and fruits and a morning walk before returning for showers and a nap for Kate. I read. In the afternoons, we walked on the beach, and even in the blustery winter winds we persisted as container ships plowed the strait out into the Pacific.

IT DIDN'T HAVE TO BE THAT WAY

During Kate's mastectomy the surgeon found a tumour eight centimetres larger than previously calculated. A lymph node biopsy revealed three nodes positive for cancer. Seeing those results, the surgeon removed fourteen more lymph nodes, a precautionary measure that soon had serious consequences.

I brought Kate home. We were home but this was never like before. The fuzzy peculiarities of something morbidly off kilter made me want more—masochistic in a way I've never indulged before.

As Kate convalesced between meetings with specialists preparing her for chemo our moments became more intimate. We compared breasts. Her right breast was twice the size of both of mine. We laughed at our prune-like nipples. She told me about breastfeeding and how she fed me six months longer than planned because our bond was so strong. When I suckled, my eyes fixed on hers, and even when I started to drifted off I battled to stay focused on my mother.

In the quiet hours, when Kate rested in the afternoons and at night, an overwhelming, intense longing made me ache. Even in my sleep. I wondered if I was ill. Trivial things were most powerful. My doll Angelica gussied up in a prom dress sat on my dresser where I left her when I walked out at eighteen. And now I slept with her tucked in my arms. I told her about Kate and my drinking and about a young boy named Rom.

Her crystal blue eyes reminded me of endless summer days as a child. And my back yard. Out there my swing waited, now a worn, haggard seat tilted slightly as if it might drop to the ground without notice. I went to it on a bleak morning in the cold rain while Kate rested. Rain turned to sleet. I was eight years old and I sat down and grabbed the ropes. I was cold and I was hot but more than anything, the feeling of flying, of freedom, it never goes away.

In Kate's bathroom, her eyeliner and lipstick, her hairbrush and even the clean towels piled neatly called to my early teens when I snuck into this room when nobody was home. I applied make-up and instantly, I was an adult. I brushed my hair to a flipped style like some of the girls in school. Jesus, I've never admitted that.

This yearning went on for days, an ache more powerful than my paranoia of tomorrow. This morning, standing in her bathroom holding her hairbrush—an opaque beauty with a wide amber handle and long dark bristles, the mirror stared back. I smirked. This isn't right. Why Kate? I'm the sicko. Leave her alone.

Kate's long hairs trailed off the brush, listing in a cold morning sun. I used this brush as a kid, trying desperately to straighten the curls so my hair could be like hers. I tried again today with the same results. I looked at myself in the mirror. Good try.

I had an awful feeling we were losing time. Kate's healing slowed. She lost weight. Was her cancer growing? Her cancer—shit. She slept mornings and afternoons. Time slid by, one week then four. She met with more doctors.

When her treatments started our routines were co-opted by a cycle of chemo every second day for three weeks, then four weeks off before another cycle sliced our lives in half. Her fatigue worsened. Too weary to work, even from home, she seldom got out of the house.

Alone for the first time in months I had an overwhelming urge to get drunk. I didn't realize how much weight I had lost. My skin, like flanks of dried beef, itched and the more I scratched the more anxious I became. I needed that high I first experienced as a teenager. Even as a kid, I knew booze owned me.

Talking about my drinking with Kate was selfish. Staying busy wasn't. I spent hours in Bolen's choosing books for her even if she didn't have the energy to read them. I shopped for fresh fruits and vegetables every afternoon. I did her banking and paid her bills. I cleaned the house, often.

And at night, alone, I worried.

Kate's bedroom morphed into her sanctuary. It overlooked the back yard and from the second floor thick oak branches created intricate weaves sparking our imaginations. Some days these branches were clumsy arms waving at people passing by and just last week Kate described them as dancers swaying rhythmically in the winter winds.

Tonight, she lay on her back with pillows propping her against the headboard. *Who Has Seen the Wind* lay unopened in her lap.

She patted the bed. "Come lie down." She winced as she flicked off the light.

I curled tight into her, close enough to inhale her soft breaths.

"Did you rest?" I asked.

"I can't. Every night is different."

I tucked the blankets under her chin. "What do you mean?"

"From the one before. As if I'm losing a little of myself."

"The surgeon did take a chunk out of your body."

She sighed.

I closed my eyes and darkness separated us and darkness fused our demons.

"Do you think I have the power to recover?"

"Many have before you. It's your turn."

"I'd like to believe I can."

She moaned. A hand went to her wound. "Hurts like hell. I've never been able sleep on my back and now it's the only position comfortable."

As sleep neared her respirations deepened. I wanted to believe she was healing, her life returning to her formal lawyering ways, on her way back to being part of my life I used to resent. I imagined each new cell replacing sick ones, bones and marrow and tissues rejuvenating. I caressed her right arm.

Our fingers entwined.

I was almost asleep when she whispered. "We've never had the best relationship."

I didn't respond.

"I've had time to think," she said.

A determined wind whistled through the crack in the open window.

"I should have been a better mother."

"Don't blame yourself."

"I'm being honest, my girl."

"I've often thought there are conversations you and I were never meant to have."

She took in a large breath, held it, then pushed it out slowly. "Mothers and daughters. Maybe that's the way it's meant to be."

"We don't have to talk about this."

"I used to think so too." Her head turned to me. "We never got along. Not properly, I mean. You've been angry since you were a teen."

"We get along fine."

"A mother worries. A mother blames herself for her child's troubles."

"I drink because I drink and I don't think you could have done anything about it."

"I'm not talking about your drinking."

My fingers pinched at her cotton nightgown.

"I'm talking about loving you just a little bit more. I should have. I wish I had."

"It's that simple?"

"Maybe."

"I kissed her cheek. You know I wasn't the easiest to get along with."

"Neither was I. It didn't have to be that way."

"Do you remember the first time Mac told you he was leaving and you invited your girlfriends over."

"You remember?"

"I was there."

"You were how old?"

"Nine. They belittled you, one, a religious nut, said it was your fault Mac left." I laughed. "She said the devil was working his ways and you had to get Mac back."

"I don't remember you being there."

"*Shelter-lady* had a baby in her arms and a black eye. She was scared as hell but she was the kindest one in the room. She never told you what to do."

"I've kept in touch with Cheryl. She's come a long way. And the baby in her arms, she's about to go to law school."

"Really?"

"Cheryl's a fighter. She's a role model for women. She did everything she could to give her children a better life."

"She haunted me for years. Stupid as it sounds I was afraid you were going to abandon me to live in a shelter."

"Not stupid at all. I only wish I knew."

"It was a silly fear. I got over it."

"Cheryl made a better life for her children than every other woman in the room."

"They belittled you."

"I was embarrassed. You were…"

"I wanted to be there for you."

"I didn't know. I'm sorry."

"I've never thanked Seth for being loyal."

"He sent me a card."

"Seth?"

"He wrote a lovely note, told me these times will pass and my memories will be of how well you took care of me. He asked if he could make anything special to eat."

She patted my shoulder. "How long have you two been going out?"

"I'm not going there."

"I'm starting to like him, Andie."

"That's nice."

"I see. This is one of *those* conversations were not meant to have?"

I turned on my side. "You don't mind if I sleep here tonight?"

"I was hoping you would."

COMPLICATIONS

It snowed overnight. A cold snap pushed down from the north over a wet city. Rain turned to ice pellets, turned to snow. A city silent. Kate's treatment session cancelled. Four inches of snow fell by early afternoon, another two by dinner. She slept through the day.

On the couch, reading *Portraits From a Wine-Stained Notebook*, I watched an ashen sky release silent flakes at first so small they seemed like motes of finely ground silk.

After dinner, a cantankerous wind wailed in the trees. Mesmerized by the transformation I went into the cold, my nostrils constricting in the arctic air. The ground crunched under my feet as wet snow leaked like a chemo drug into a fragile earth. When I drank, it was wine that defiled me, numbed my emotions, made me inhuman, gave me release. Now, alone without a crutch, I needed Kate more than ever.

I zipped my coat and I went for a walk. This wasn't the Kate I always believed would be there—wistful words from a troubled-life bitch. I ached for the stupidity of my moral high ground during those ridiculous arguments with her. Even the feelings of frustration when I knew she was right seemed quaint. We were vibrant. We battled.

I had nobody now. Seth had moved on. The night he told me about his dream of us walking on a frosted field—our moment but I never told him how much it meant to me.

We worked with a nutritionist to identify a suitable diet to keep Kate eating. She picked at her food, lost more weight, slept day and night. She asked me to contact Seth so he might come over and cook a meal for us. I lied. I told her Seth was working on a menu list that he would soon share.

On her bathroom floor that morning I found large clumps of Kate's hair. I picked up her hairbrush, it too was a tangle of mats. As I plucked hair from the brush I couldn't help think about the simple act of brushing—reassuring, reinforcing a self-long established habit. And now this most reassuring of habits was tainted with disease, a diesease spreading inside her.

Soon after completing the chemo Kate's left arm and hand started to swell. The lymph fluid had nowhere to drain, leading to lymphedema, a common side effect of breast cancer where lymph nodes have been removed. A physical therapist recommended Kate wear a specialized glove on her hand to help reduce the swelling. Her arm continued to swell. After the glove, we tried wraps designed for lymphedema treatment. When that didn't work, a compression sleeve was recommended.

Lymphedema was shit, a constant reminder of the disease. The pain in her upper arm arced into her wrist and fingers. She couldn't work. Self-conscious of her swollen limb, embarrassed that everyone would look at her, she stayed inside. I told her it didn't matter what others thought. I enticed her walk the beach where we tucked our chins into the cold winds, walked slow, said little. Kate didn't last long. I had to help her up the slope onto the road where she rested. Her pink cheeks were an illusion. Each time, arm in arm, I guided her home.

Finally, this treatment cycle was over. Would there be more? I had never seen her so calm. She never liked to wait. Now waiting was as much a part of the day as the pain. She accepted both with grace. When she winced, her eyes closed and her face scrunched up. Sometimes to fight the pain she stopped breathing and I would touch her arm and her eyes opened. As I leaned in and kissed her forehead she repeated the same thing each time.

"Hold me, Andie."

I wrapped her in my arms. We heard each other breathe and listened silently to our hopes because we still had them but never shared them. In the afternoons, she stared into the back yard for hours while I made her tea that she never drank. I sometimes fell asleep next to her only to be woken by a kiss.

I enjoyed shopping for her. At the drug store to pick up her prescriptions I waited patiently at the check-out. Patiently? A few months ago I tried to throttle a clerk when he said he couldn't find my cellphone. This afternoon the clerk asked me if there was anything else I needed. I shook my head. Didn't need to tell her that I wanted only one thing. *Yeah, I do need something—how about restoring Kate back to health.*

The clerk tucked the bottles in a bag and I headed out. As I walked towards the exit I spotted Jaymie walking towards me.

"Jaymie."

She spun around. "Andie!" She giggled as she came to me. We hugged in the doorway as others skirted around us.

"What are you doing here?"

I showed her the bag. "Prescriptions."

Her brow furrowed. "I'm so sorry. How is she?"

She didn't let me answer.

"Andie, I've missed you." She wrung my hands and wouldn't let go. "I've been worried."

"I'm better."

"The night at the restaurant, when you ran…"

"You know me."

"And Kate?"

"She's not well."

"And you're taking care of her. How great is that."

"Crazy as it is, I'm glad." I hesitated. "So… you've seen Seth?"

"A couple weeks ago. He bought me coffee."

"I see."

"You haven't seen him?"

"Oh no, been busy, you know… How's Rom?"

"He had another seizure."

My gut twisted. "Is he ok?"

"Seth says he's fine but will need to take the medications Melissa thought were unnecessary."

"I miss Rom."

Her cheeks tightened. "You know life would be a lot simpler if you two just moved in together. You could take care of Rom."

"We're just friends. We—"

"Don't. Seth's a great fit and you know it."

She squeaked, "I miss you."

We moved out into the cold. Her red cheeks and bright blue eyes, this was the Jaymie I knew.

She couldn't contain herself. "I'm seeing someone." She giggled.

"What?"

"I know. Hey, come to dinner. I'll tell you all about him."

"Where did you meet him?"

"He's a neighbour two doors down. He lost his wife two years ago to canc—." She stopped herself. "Oh, God…"

"We can't pretend."

"Hey, the kids and I are back home. John moved out after Christmas."

"How are they?"

"Much better. I even enjoy dealing with teenage fears. You'll come to dinner?"

"As long as Brent isn't there."

She roared. "I'm so sorry."

"You have no idea."

She started towards the parking lot. "I'll text. We'll set something up."

I waved as snow began to fall on a gelid winter afternoon.

Energized by my encounter with Jaymie, I wrote Seth a letter. I had to know about Rom, about the new medications and how he was doing at school. I told him about Kate. It was strange writing to him after all these months. I tried to remain distant but the words fell easily on to the page and I worried I might be sending the wrong message.

I had another reason to write. On separate pages, I laid out my transgressions, the unexpurgated version of the years we hung out, the egregious trysts and dispirited rants, reminding Seth of those times I crushed him just to please myself. He needed to know the real Andie, and be under no illusion we could be happy after all the things I've done. I was specific—the times I drank when he thought I was sober, the lies he knew nothing about—that I had been fired from my teaching job, how I used him in Tofino as a shield from my dysfunctional parents, that I made out with Brent and tried to seduce Mitch.

He had to know these things.

A NEW SEASON

As time crawled away from us Kate became a physical part of me. When her breaths were shallow and erratic, so were mine. I wrapped my hands around hers to keep her warm. I watched her restless struggles to sleep—head turning, mouth agape, a body fighting, a spirit fading. Each night I crawled into bed beside her. Always cold, she never complained. A growing nausea competed with the painful lymphedema.

Mind and body, hers and mine—we were losing the battle. Her cancer metastasized further into her lymph nodes and her chest wall. Stage IIIB they said. Marathons of radiation treatments took over. Numbing routines. I was a bitch with nurses and doctors. Their soft words of encouragement pissed me off, they were symbols of futility. Desperation without options is ugly. I watched staff walk away after their shifts and I hated them.

Gestures, inflections, mine were Kate's. A soft smile, hands folded on tummies, headshakes instead of words. Fatigue. I lived inside her. I retched when she retched. When her abdomen cramped and she could barely breathe and she didn't make it to bathroom on time I cleaned up. Kate was embarrassed. Shit on the floor was real and cleaning up was something I could do.

I bought her new sheets, new fuzzy pajamas and expensive face washes and soft thick towels. We slept beside each other in her bed, sometimes in mine.

I wore the same jeans and sweatshirt every day. Combing my hair back in the morning, I didn't bother with makeup. Rarely showered. Why look after myself. If Kate was dying so was I. One morning I looked at myself in the mirror. This is what decay looks like. I had a choice. Kate didn't. Guilt came calling. Was I wrong to desire a young woman's body, the body I once owned, vibrant, supple, aching to the touch of a loved one? It was selfish, I know. I confessed to Kate. She laughed. She told me it was fine if I acquired a young woman's body as long as my mind stayed forty-one.

Grief started slowly. A faint unease gained momentum in the early hours of the day. I couldn't sleep. Started thinking—dark thoughts of more trips to doctors, sitting in waiting rooms until we were ushered in to receive more bad news we never wanted to hear. I was losing her. Usually, I drink when I lose control.

Instead, I panicked. What the hell were we doing wasting time on a cycle of endless sessions that didn't work? Kate was worse. I had to do something.

Most people see grief as something to be purged with a how-to book. Grief isn't something to be learned. It's seldom linear, it always hurts. But we don't talk about loss, do we? If a relationship comes apart, if a marriage fails, if a mom is painfully ill with cancer—we don't talk about it. Rousseau wrote, *"He who pretends to look on death without fear, lies. All men are afraid of dying, this is the great law of sentient beings, without which the entire human species would soon be destroyed."*

But Rousseau's days are distant and unfamiliar with humans today. We believe we can live, if not forever, decades longer, into our eighties and nineties. Death is invisible so grief must be too.

When Seth raised the topic of death, when we discussed *The Scream*, I dismissed him.

I began to think it was easier to make peace with my own mortality than Kate's. I hated myself. What spirit I held in these last few months, if not for Kate, was dead. I could die today and that would be all. But Kate—a primal fear like Seth's ripped through me whenever I thought about losing her. *I'm sorry, Seth. I didn't understand. I do now.*

Kate's death would terminate a bond between mother and child that began inside the mother's womb. I struggled to find a reason for my life. Who was I? Why am I here? I can drink. Is that what I'm supposed to do? The only thing I've ever done well is hate myself.

If Kate died who would take care of me? Maybe it would be better if I went with her. Wouldn't it be better than going back to the bottle and blackouts and the debasing things I'd do? How many others would I assault like I did the night I punched Seth and ripped his shirt, or the insanity of charging into an emergency room and striking the security guards as I fought my way to see Rom—how soon would I be there again?

Until recently, we walked the half-acre property every morning. Kate insisted. She strolled with her hands behind her back, wearing one winter sweater over another and gloves but no coat, leaning over every bed searching for signs of spring. Daffodils and snowdrops poked up from the wet earth. Soon their flowers would follow. This became important. Intimate, even in the rain. We knew what we were doing, we laughed at our efforts to find signs of the new season when we both knew it was hope we were looking for.

Terror sweats at night came calling, agonizing fears about losing Kate. I threw off my covers. I walked for miles under cold, white stars.

I resented a system that saw Kate as no different than any other patient. She was different. I had to fix this. What was I thinking? What the hell was wrong with me? I decided to take her to the States or Mexico or the Philippines, wherever necessary, where experimental drugs and treatments made a difference for patients. We were running out of time.

As I came into the house just before five one morning I realized yesterday was my birthday. Shit, happy forty-two. Kate called from the bedroom. She lay on the bed, shivering, unable to get up. Her blankets scattered on the floor.

As I gathered them up she said, "I can't pee. It hurts."

We raced down the highway in the ambulance. I sat at her side. We held hands. Her tired eyes stayed on me, a mother the child, the child again the mother.

As the ambulance backed in to the emergency ward she whispered, "Mac's coming to see me on the weekend."

"What?"

"He's going to be disappointed if nobody is home."

"What are you talking about?"

"He's coming to visit."

"When?"

"Friday."

"I don't understand."

"I don't have to tell you all my secrets." She closed her eyes and winced. The attendant told Kate to rest.

She stayed in hospital for five days until the bladder infection cleared. Cancer progressed. The oncologist suggested more radiation. Kate wasn't sure. He suggested that they could mitigate the pain with different medications. Kate asked if she could wait a few days for a decision.

Wait for what?

After the doctor left Kate asked me to sit with her.

"You're upset."

"You need the radiation. What else can—"

"Andie, I have to do this on my terms. I have to be ready regardless of my choices."

Tears welled up. I couldn't stop.

Mac visited. This was surreal. I witnessed tender gestures of warm compresses on Kate's forehead, he helped her into clean pajamas, went on errands and bought her snacks of chocolate and wine gums. When he massaged her feet, he told me the story of the time they first dated, how they walked for miles around campus until she grew tired. He got her to lie down and with his back against a massive oak he massaged her feet while Kate rambled on about her high school years and the losers she dated.

When she rested, Mac and I walked. Spring arrived. A warming sun helped to dismiss dark images in my mind.

"Why did you stay away when you knew she had cancer?"

"I didn't know, not right away. Not until last month. She called. We texted but she knows I don't text. I wanted to come right away. She said no. She wanted to be sure my visits were not sympathy visits."

"She said that?"

"She said that's one of the reasons she's loved having you back," he chuckled, "she knows you don't feel sorry for her."

Across the field a father and son, the boy about ten, were playing catch with a football. The boy tried but every time the ball came his way he dropped it. I could hear the father encouraging, ever patient, telling his son the next catch would be his. I ached.

Mac interrupted. "Kate wants us to rebuild."

"What?"

"I never wanted us separate. I know you won't believe me. I've been a fool at times. I've betrayed Kate."

"Well, if you're talking imperfections then I can probably best you if you want to compare."

"You probably don't know this but I haven't signed the divorce papers."

"Does she know?"

"She knows."

"Jesus. I'm stunned. I don't know what to say."

"Let's take it slowly for now. Let's take care of your mom."

"She wants this too?"

"She does. She told me you're keeping her alive. She was making progress until last month."

I was caustic. "Until the dying disease spread."

"I had to see her. Our phone conversations, something happened. When we first met, every word mattered. It's like that again." He smiled. "Things she said, the way she laughed when I told her about how often I forget things. We laughed about sleeping alone but out of habit we still reached over to hold on to someone no longer there. She reminded me when we were young she would get up early in the mornings and make coffee and breakfast and send me off to class with a kiss on the forehead—we're in love again."

He looked down at me. "How did you not hear our conversations?"

"Kate says you talked in the afternoons. I'm usually out running errands."

A chuckle rumbled.

"What?"

"You're happy."

My head shook. "I don't know. I really don't. But Kate and I are stronger in ways we never thought."

"I've heard."

"Jesus, you two do keep secrets."

"Not secrets. We're parents."

"Are you staying long?"

"I have to go to California for a few days. I'll be back next week. I'm going to ask Kate if I can come home."

He smiled the smile I loved as a child.

"You sure about this?"

"I am. And you and I, we haven't talked enough."

"Not since Tofino last summer."

He stopped. "I sold my interest in my companies in the fall."

"No, you didn't…"

"I did. I travel now to provide advice to entrepreneurs. I'm enjoying myself but I'm slowing down. I'm tired."

I never thought of Mac as tired. Those blue eyes were always full of drive and ambition but around the corners of his mouth hard lines of regret lingered.

"Can you make it work this time?"

"I know we can."

HUMANITY'S BETTER ANGELS

Mac returned earlier than expected. He was determined to bring Kate home. She wasn't ready. The pain in her lower back was unbearable so the doctors increased the morphine and Kate went on a high recounting stories of teenage years with a zeal that made everyone smile, stories I'd never heard before. Even Mac laughed at renditions much saltier than the originals.

Most of the time she rested, Mac and I at her side. We talked quietly, caught up on the last year. When Mac's phone buzzed and he stepped out into the hallway, Kate's eyes opened. I told her he would be back soon.

The only other patient in Kate's room was an elderly man whose Alzheimer's had taken him from his family. He was oblivious to his colon cancer. His wife, always there, was joined each night by generations of family members where loud conversations rambled back and forth with no beginnings, no ends. They bitched about the Canucks. The elders asked about Netflix and how it worked and when it came to local politics tempers flared about what to do with street people camping in city parks.

It was almost like the old man wasn't there. His blankets remained unruffled, his hands motionless at his sides. But I noticed his eyelids flickered whenever a salient remark sparked a distant mind.

And each night, when it was time for family to leave, the old man's eyes opened. A gentle smile creased his face as grandchildren bent to kiss his forehead, leaving him with the similar reminders, "Love you, Pappa," and "Don't try and run away, we know where to find you."

Mac, Kate and I were a small and wavering family compared to this clan. One of us had cancer. One was in his seventies and the other a barren forty-two-year-old cynic who until recently drank for a living. Our prospects for future generations were slim and fading.

If Kate was the only patient on the floor these nurses couldn't have been more caring. I choked up when one of them fussed around her this afternoon—tidying blankets, replacing pillows with fresh, clean ones, reminding Kate she would be home and comfy in her own bed in a few days. It wasn't this nurse on this shift. They were all like this.

These men and women who witness so much misery moved from one patient to another as if guided by humanity's better angels. It was in the quiet of the night when the lights were out that their devotions, yes that's what I called them, were spiritual—gentle hands, soothing whispers, ever on the lookout to assist they moved silently from one patient to another. How they managed to stay resilient shift after shift I don't know. I wouldn't last a day.

Kate went home when the medications lessened the pain enough for her to be able to move around. At home, we tried to make her comfortable, always seeking the right balance between respecting her independence—her will to chart her own path by not over-stepping on matters of privacy, yet there to attend to pragmatic needs like helping her dress and undress. She laughed at her frailties. She never complained. Always grateful for sunshine and clean sheets and new pajamas; when I bought her a new pair of slippers, she wept.

It was us three. Mac, genuinely interested in my life, asked questions I had no answers to. I told him about my past, about my drinking. He didn't know. He didn't judge. He was impressed I abandoned my addiction to care for Kate. I told him it was something I could do.

In the mornings, Kate and Mac strolled in the back yard. Spring, in blossom, soothed us with warm winds. Mac took the opportunity to gather a handful of lilacs for an impromptu bouquet. When Kate tired, they rested on the wicker chairs on the front deck. Later, she slept with Mac at her side, his arm around her.

She wasn't home long. Intolerable pain returned. This time in her back. Her breathing erratic, at times short heaving breaths forced her to gasp. Other times her breaths were inaudible. Mac called an ambulance. He sat with her on the way to hospital.

She endured more tests and scans. We waited through the afternoon into the night until the next morning when we were summoned to Kate's bed. Dr. Richards, a big boned woman with rich, dark eyes carried herself with the grace of a dancer. She spoke in an easy, relaxed manner when she told us Kate's cancer had spread to her spine.

I barely heard her words. My mind hummed exhaustion.

I stared at Kate's bristled hair, hair only six months ago lustrous and long. How odd a skull looks when exposed. How fragile. It was the want in her eyes—desperate appeals for more time, for her hand in mine, and sunshine on her face, sweet, sweet mundanities.

Dr. Richards spoke to me. "The pain will occur mostly when Kate is moving. It's a mechanical pain, indicating the tumour is causing weakness or instability in the bones of the spine."

She paused. "It's good for her to walk because her adrenal glands make steroids during the day and this will lessen the pain." She continued. "I would suggest we proceed with radiation."

Kate nodded.

I rejected the idea of cancer in her spine. Radiation? This was too fucking much. What the hell were we doing to her? Radiation? How was that going to help?

Mac saw my frustration. He guided me out of the room. "It's not your fault."

"It's not right. Shit. Shit. What are they doing to her?"

"Look, I know you—"

"Don't belittle me."

"I wasn't. We *have* to do the radiation."

"And how is that supposed to help?"

"I know, but we have to, Andie."

I turned away. "It makes me so fuckin' mad." I released his hand on my arm. "I'm going for a walk."

Anger burned a laser hole in me. In the parking lot, I swore and screamed until my lungs burst. I kicked a shiny SUV parked too close to my rage. Jesus, what did they expect from her? Was she supposed to shrug and say, *Hell ya, give me more drugs. Give me more pain.* When was she allowed to cry out?

It's impossible to make this shit up. Month after month of diagnosis and treatment and more bad news as we stumbled into darkness. I wasn't sure I could go back inside and face her. How was she going to get through this? How? What would I say to her? *It's ok Kate, it's only more cancer.*

"Andie?"

Lost in my rage I didn't see him. His familiar voice forced me to spin around.

"Andie, it's me."

"Seth?"

I babbled. "What are you doing here? What are you…?"

"Kate asked me to come visit."

He beamed.

"No, she didn't." I was confused. Seth looked great. Words tumbled out of my mouth. "Kate's cancer has spread. It's bad. She needs more radiation. I don't know if it's too late. She's in a lot of pain. Mac's home. They're together again."

"I know."

"What?"

"Let's go see Kate."

"Where's Rom?"

"With his care-giver."

I was nervous in the elevator. My mind reeled. Kate's dying? What's Seth doing here? I charged out when the door opened. Seth followed and as I entered Kate's room I stopped fast. Mac leaned over her touching the rim of her ear with the tip of his baby finger. He whispered.

I started to turn around when Seth bumped into me.

"Whoa." I grabbed his hand and yanked him into the hallway.

He stood over me. "Hi."

"Just so you know I'm having a shitty day."

"I can't imagine." He pulled me in kissing my forehead.

"It's too much, Seth. Almost a year of this of shit and now more cancer."

"She told me you've been amazing."

"I'm doing what any child would do."

"I wouldn't want to get in your way."

"I'm exhausted. I won't say anything to Kate. How could I? She's a monster. You can't imagine what she's put up with."

"Kate said you've done everything possible."

"It's not enough. All I want to do is scoop her up and run away from all this fucking insanity."

"I'm so sorry."

I looked at him again. He looked good. Really, good.

"Kate says you've been taking care of yourself."

"I'm as thin as ever. I try to fix myself up but what for? You know me."

"Still charting your distant self away from this world."

"This fucked up world."

He laughed that ten-year-old laugh of his and instantly I felt Rom.

"There's been only one benefit."

His eyebrows flickered.

I had to tell him. "I've been so busy taking care of Kate, I haven't had a single drink."

"So that's the solution."

I laughed hard. "Who knew…"

"I hope you're not upset about me being here."

"Wait… Kate told you Mac's home?"

"I came by last week. You were out picking up meds."

"You came by the house?"

"Rom too."

"No!" I shrieked.

He shook his head. "I wouldn't do that to you."

He turned us around towards Kate's room. We walked slowly holding on to each other's words.

"Why didn't you tell Jaymie we're no longer together?"

"Because it's not true." His arm crooked inside mine and we stopped. "Besides, Kate said you and I should see more of each other."

"Did she?"

"But I want you to decide. I'll do whatever you want."

"I'm a wreck, Seth. I can't right now."

"Not today. You don't have to decide today."

IT'S NOT EASY TO EXPLAIN

Insistent rays pushed through diaphanous myrtle green oak leaves warming the earth, enticing me outside. I sat on the bench underneath the apple tree of my childhood. Finches and robins sang out to their mates and the sun on my face called me skyward. I squinted. With all the things going on with Kate the perfection in the moment reminded me I had relearned to feel. Of course, feeling meant confronting the revulsion I still had for myself. I dared not think too much.

Taking care of Kate mattered. Radiation treatments cut through her weakened body. Our lives altered course again. She apologized for the mess. Mouth sores made it impossible for her to eat. Her clothes dwarfed a bony skeleton. She smiled sadness.

Some days were better. When a whiff of energy took hold she poked her nose into Mac's crossword. They bantered possibilities, scratching in answers until fatigue forced her to lie down. One morning as I ate breakfast she shuffled into the kitchen and leaned against the doorway.

"When are you going back to work?"

"I'm not leaving until the cancer is gone."

"You have to rebuild your life. Go back to your teaching at the university."

I shrugged. "I will when the time is right."

She slept a lot. At times, deep, peaceful sleeps made me think her body was healing. I dared to hope. Other times, restless, she woke cranky and out of sorts. Mac and I thought she had grown stronger under our care. We also knew self-delusion is a solid defence against the truth.

The flower and vegetable beds were a mess. Abandoned since fall the warm winter and early spring allowed weeds to overrun. The raspberries were tangled, unpruned and drowning in undergrowth. The four feet tall canes sprouted to open spaces.

I grabbed a few hand tools from the shed, a pair of leather gloves and settled in under the canes as I soaked up an afternoon sun.

I'd forgotten about the soothing benefits of quiet labour. I worked my way along the first row, at first pulling fistfuls of weeds before tending to the determined stragglers. Behind me mounds of creepers, dandelions and an assortment of invaders wilted in the sun.

I had just taken my fleece off when I noticed Kate walking towards me. Wrapped in a woolen blanket, a navy toque plastered to her head, her childlike crooked half-smile made me laugh. She rested on the bench, her voice weak. "I saw you out here. I want to watch."

"You can help. I'm not sure I'm getting all the weeds out."

"I think you know what you are doing."

"How are you and Mac doing?" I asked.

Kate absorbed the question. "It's like we're dating for the first time. Except now we know ourselves better than when we were young." She paused. "It feels reassuring to have lived a few good years, fought and fallen away, and now we're together again. It's not easy to explain."

Most days Mac puttered around the house, something he had never done. He repaired loose spindles on the banister and tightened hinges on the kitchen cupboards. He read a lot. Most of the time he sat with Kate. He seemed, I don't know, content.

"You and Mac, all the troubles, and the leaving and coming back and the threats of divorce—you stayed together."

"I know. It's not what I thought. I'm happy, Andie."

"Mac too."

A bunch of long shoots dangled from my hand. "What's this?"

"Horsetails."

"They're everywhere." I tossed them onto the pile.

"Are you enjoying getting your hands dirty?"

"I have to admit it feels good."

"You used to help me when you were a child."

"I still don't know the names of most weeds."

"We stayed together… somehow we knew even if the threads were worn our relationship was strong enough to hold."

"Enough to go to Tofino every year."

"Enough you wanted to be there. Even a disengaged young woman knew where she belonged."

"I sometimes wonder if those times in Tofino are the reason I'm here now."

"Maybe." She pulled the toque over her ears. "But I also know you made your mind up a long time ago to go your own way."

"Didn't get far."

A painful smile emerged then fell away.

"What I don't understand was why you had to go and get sick?"

"It was part of the plan to get you back."

"And this, what is it?"

"Buttercup. And those taller, spikier weeds…"

I pointed, "These?"

"Those are stinging nettles."

Kate leaned against the armrest.

"Do you want to go in?"

"Not yet."

"Let me know and I'll make you a cup of tea."

She nodded.

Not only was she coping with cancer, Kate was a mother helping her daughter find her way again. All these years and I underestimated her. She couldn't hide the pleasure of her matchmaking. I was too overwhelmed to make sense of Seth. Maybe I was pleased about seeing him. Maybe I wanted to see him again.

I glanced back. She studied me.

"What?" I asked.

"Walk me inside. I'd like that cup of tea now."

After dinner Mac and I were watching TV when Kate sat down. She was restless. She stared at the TV then looked around aimlessly, confused. She studied me, as if she didn't know me.

"Kate?"

She looked over at Mac.

"Everything ok?" he asked.

She didn't answer. Her brow furrowed when she asked. "How was teaching today?"

"What do you mean?"

Mac intervened. "Andie didn't—?"

"You told me this morning you had class."

"No, I..." I tried not to react.

She pointed to the wall. "I don't remember when the bookshelves were so full of books. They were empty until yesterday."

"Empty?"

"Yes, empty. What did you think I meant?" She turned away in frustration.

Mac raised himself from the chair and walked from the room. I waited until Kate's attention turned to the TV and slipped out.

"Something's happened," he said.

"It's too late today to call her doctor."

"We'll call her in the morning."

Dr. Borden listened quietly as I described the events of last night. She asked if there was anything different about Kate this morning. "Yes," I said. "She couldn't find her way downstairs without Mac helping."

"Ok, then. I want you to take her to emergency."

"Now?" I asked stupidly.

"Andie, something's going on and we're going to find out."

I rode with her this time. She stared at me with eyes both inquisitive and trusting. She held my hand. The medic began placing an oxygen mask on her face. She lifted her head and the mask slid into place.

"Better?" I asked.

"I'm getting used to this." She patted my hand. "Where are we going?"

"There are doctors waiting at the hospital. They'd like to see you."

"Do you think they've missed me?" Her eyes flickered resilience.

WE'RE GOOD THEN

We never talked about Kate dying. The topic slid by as time slipped away. All these months she battled and battled and not once did we broach the topic. I couldn't do it. But this morning as she was wheeled through emergency she waved and the gurney went around the corner, I couldn't help wonder if this was her time.

Emotions flooded. Disbelief, anger. *Jesus, not now, Kate.*

It's odd the things you think about. In grade six my best friend Beth announced she was moving to Winnipeg at the end of the school year. Why? My first reaction, denial. Beth's not moving. She can't. She's my best friend. I was angry. How could she? She cried. I cried. I decided I wasn't going to make friends with anyone, anymore.

In the fall after Beth left, Alice arrived. Alice was as confused as me. Maybe that's why we got along.

And when the Hatter asked what day of the month it was and Alice said the fourth. The Hatter sighed and said, 'Two days wrong.' Alice thought it was a funny watch, 'It tells the day of the month but doesn't tell what o'clock it is. 'Why should it?' muttered the Hatter. 'Does your watch tell you what year it is?'

My fingers tapped my phone.

"Andie." Mac rested a hand on mine. "They've taken Kate for a MRI. They said we should wait."

"MRI?"

"For her brain, I think."

Across from us a mother around my age sat next to her son. The boy, maybe fourteen, cupped his left arm at the wrist. His ashen face flinched when he pulled the arm to his ribs. He saw me watching, his eyes darted to the floor. His mother whispered. His head shook in embarrassment. Her hand caressed. His head shook.

Mac paced. Another round of tests and consultations was better than the alternative. I know. Whatever we could do to keep her alive, whatever sacrifices I needed to make, it was worth it. To hell with tomorrow. Fuck it. Fuck Kate getting better. She only needed to survive today.

A nurse came by in the early afternoon. Petite and businesslike she informed us Kate had been moved upstairs. More tests were planned. We could go see her now.

I was consumed. With Kate. Keeping her alive. I could do this. We could do this. And get out of my way. I'm going to lock myself inside her room, just the two of us and I'm going kiss her hands and lay on that skinny bed and rub her back, and remind her we're going to be ok. We're going to be ok. We will be ok.

We were almost at Kate's room when I spotted Seth in the doorway of her room.

I mumbled. "How did you know we were here?"

"You texted me."

When Dr. Richards floated into the room we didn't notice at first. She moved to the bed and looked down at Kate.

"Hi, Doc." Kate tried to sit up but couldn't.

"How are you feeling?"

"Oh, you know, bad news has a way of perking me up."

Dr. Richards couldn't hide a smile. Her rich brown eyes looked around the bed at us. "I have some good news and some not so good news."

"Do tell," Kate insisted.

"From the MRI and our early analysis we have determined that you have a tumour on your brain."

"Wonderful. Wonderful." Kate's glazed eyes hinted resentment. "Did you hear that? I have a tumour on my brain."

The doctor kept her words brief. "It may well be a metastatic tumour related to your breast cancer."

"Isn't this lovely news?"

I was surprised how much Kate sounded like me.

"I'm sorry, Kate." The doctor glanced around the room and back to Kate. "The reality is women like you are surviving breast cancer longer than ever. This means that cancer can spread to other parts of the body."

"Including the brain?" Mac asked.

"Including the brain."

Kate smirked. "So I'm one of the lucky ones."

"In a sense, yes. We have yet to confirm the tumour is cancerous."

"And you think it started in the breast?" I asked.

"We do."

Mac kissed Kate on the forehead and looked at Dr. Richards. "If it is cancer, is it treatable?"

"It depends on the type of tumour and since we don't know enough now we'll monitor the tumour for changes using a series of MRIs or CT scans."

"Oh, this is good. More trips to clinics and time with my friends in health care."

Dr. Richards smiled warmly. "Your brain's a tricky piece of real estate. We need to proceed cautiously. The MRIs and CTs are excellent tools that will assist us with next steps."

"Which are?" I interjected.

"The tumour may be located at the control centre for thought, emotion and movement. That can affect an individual's physical and cognitive abilities and quality of life."

She looked at Mac. "That's probably what you witnessed last night and again this morning."

"Will my brain require surgery?"

"First a biopsy and then surgery if the tumour is operable."

"And then?"

"Radiation or chemo. It depends what we find."

Kate adjusted herself and then looked around the room. "You realize after what I've been through there's not a lot left to find."

"I respectfully disagree. And look at these people with you. They're ready to do whatever they can on your behalf."

"They've given me a reason to get out of bed."

Dr. Richards looked at me. "It's a hell of a battle. It's good to be angry."

"Oh, shit. Am I ever. I'm sorry, Kate."

"I'm angry too, my girl."

The doctor added. "If it helps I can lend you any extra I have." She stood up. "If you will excuse me I have to see another patient. I'll be back shortly. If you have any questions I can answer them then."

All those years I treated Kate like shit. I laughed in her face. I rebuffed all her attempts to get close. The truth is I ridiculed her more than her so-called friends.

I kissed her on the cheek. "I'm going for a walk."

Seth was right behind me. He brought me to a stop at the elevator.

I couldn't look at him. "Don't," I said.

"What?"

"Don't say... anything."

I vibrated. And burst. "I came home to do something. For once in my fucking life I tried to do something good."

"You did. You are."

"Kate and I, we were finding our way. And then cancer comes along and fucks everything up."

"Not everything."

I leaned into him, his chest warm against my cheek. "The tumour on her brain is operable. How fucking nice."

"We'll take care of her. I want to help if you will let me."

"I'm not sure if I have anything left."

"You do."

"I'm not sure I can do this—you and I, I mean."

"We can."

"I want to." I looked into his eyes.

"Me too. And Rom."

"I'm probably going to drink."

A hand stroked the back of my head.

"I'm going to betray you."

"I'll be there."

"And hurt you more than I have in the past."

"I will do my best to forgive."

If I drink, I'll pick up where I left off. You understand?"

"I do."

"And for Rom, are you worried about having a drunk in your home?"

"Our home."

"Doesn't it worry you?"

"Of course."

His lips touched mine.

I pulled away.

"I'm still a selfish bitch."

"My bitch."

"Oh, Jesus."

"We'll do this together."

I looked at him.

"What?"

"I meant to ask you something."

His fingers entwined inside my curls.

"Did you read the note I sent you a few weeks ago?"

"Some of it."

"Some?"

"I read the beginning. You told me about Kate." He reached into his wallet.

"Not all of it?"

"No."

"Why?"

"It wasn't important."

"Why?"

The note rested between his fingers.

"Well?" My heart pounded.

"You think I need to know the sordid details of your past?"

"I do."

"I don't."

"Because?"

"Because your transgressions are yours, Andie Burrows. I have a pretty good idea of what went on behind my back."

My mouth was dry. "Don't you want to know?"

"No."

"I don't understand."

"If it helps, you should feel good about coming clean."

"It's not enough. I want you to love me for all I am."

Seth stood back. "What did you just say?"

My face crimsoned.

"It makes no difference if I read the note. Do you understand?"

"I'm trying, Seth. I'm trying."

"We're good then?"

"Oh no, we're far from good. But it's time we took a run at making this work."

He flipped the note into the trash bin outside Kate's room. "It's interesting, isn't it?"

"What is?"

"Like Kate and Mac, you and I are incapable of going our separate ways."

CPSIA information can be obtained
at www.ICGtesting.com
Printed in the USA
LVOW07s0609310517
536362LV00001B/145/P